SKINNY DIPPING

A band of horsemen was crossing the ford.

"We'd better get our clothes on and get out of here," Farnam said.

"We don't have time," Jessie snapped. "Come on, Joe! Let's hit them now before they see us!"

Her movement caught the eye of one of the riders. A shout rang out as she reached, naked, for her rifle.

"Damn!" Farnam leaped past Jessie to get his own gun. "We've got a fight on our hands now!"

LONE STAR

Also in the LONE STAR series
from Jove

WESLEY ELLIS

LONE STAR

AND THE
BORDER BANDITS

A JOVE BOOK

LONE STAR AND THE BORDER BANDITS

A Jove Book / published by arrangement with
the author

PRINTING HISTORY
Jove edition / September 1982
Fourth printing / June 1983

ISBN: 0-515-07540-X

Jove books are published by The Berkley Publishing Group,
200 Madison Avenue, New York, N.Y. 10016.
The words "A JOVE BOOK" and the "J" with sunburst
are trademarks belonging to Jove Publications, Inc.

PRINTED IN THE UNITED STATES OF AMERICA

Chapter 1

"You don't really need to ride the fencelines today, Ki," Jessie Starbuck said. "I'm sure Ed's kept everything in good shape while we were gone."

"Of course he has," Ki agreed. "Ed's a good strawboss. I never worry when he's in charge while we're away."

"Then rest today, Ki," Jessie suggested. "The fence will still be there tomorrow."

"Oh, I'm not tired, Jessie." Ki paused and added, "Besides, when I ride line, I see more than the barbwire. I see the sun and the sky and the range." He lowered his head for a moment and then looked up at Jessie again, his dark eyes glowing between the almond-shaped ovals of their lids. "Sometimes I even think I see more than what I'm looking at. Does that make sense to you?"

"Yes," Jessie replied thoughtfully.

She understood Ki's need for an occasional period of solitude. Line-riding gave him time to meditate with the Japanese half of his ancestry and to reconcile it with the American half. Her eyes swept the broad, ridge-broken range that stretched in a seemingly endless expanse away from the buildings and horse corrals of the Circle Star. In the slanting light of the early-morning sun, the sparse prairie grasses that covered the earth rippled gently in response to the small breeze.

Without looking at Ki, Jessie went on, "Alex taught me that there's a lot more to this place than someone can take in at a glance."

"You're sure you don't want to go with me?"

"No. I'm going to stay here this time. Besides..."

Ki nodded when Jessie stopped short. Just as Jessie understood his feelings, Ki grasped what she did not want to put into words. Riding the fenceline would take him past the ravine where Alex Starbuck had died, cut down by a hail of bullets from the guns of a band of hired assassins. Even now, the place of her father's death was still the one spot on the ranch that Jessie avoided going near.

"I'll be back in plenty of time for supper," he said. He lifted one hand in a half-wave, half-salute as he wheeled his horse and started at a fast walk away from the corral.

During the periods when both he and Jessie were at the ranch, Ki took his duties as foreman very seriously, and on any Texas ranch in the 1880s, keeping fences in shape was a job that had no end. Though barbwire had been in use for several years before Alex Starbuck began fencing the Circle Star range, it was widely disliked.

In the time that had passed since then, barbwire had gained respect, but no liking. Fences were still cut by trail-drive hands, who resented the detours they had to make around what had been open range. Footloose cowpunchers in search of jobs snipped the strands so they could travel in a straight line from ranch to ranch. Rustlers cut big sections out of fences when they were making off with a stolen herd.

Ki counted himself lucky when he'd ridden half the morning without having to tighten a sagging strand or splice a cut. He'd made mental notes of two or three skewed fence-posts that would need attention later, but his ride had been uninterrupted until he saw that company was ahead.

Less than three miles away, where a solitary mesquite bush had struggled through enough dry summers to attain the status of a tree, a half-dozen cowhands were riding across the range. Their course was at a right angle to the Circle Star fence. Ki looked along the line of wire; even at that distance he could see where the barbwire strands sagged to the ground between two of the widely spaced posts that separated Starbuck range from that of its south-

2

western neighbor, the Lazy G. Touching his toe to the flank of his horse, Ki speeded up.

It was obvious to Ki that if he could see the Lazy G hands, they could see him. Holding his irritation in check, he followed the custom of the country and waved a greeting to the riders. When he received no wave in reply, Ki frowned and toed his mount into a distance-eating lope.

He'd covered half the distance to the approaching band when the riders veered suddenly and headed for the old mesquite. Ki saw that he was too far away to cut off the trespassers before they reached the tree, and he changed his direction to meet them. The cowhands were closer to the mesquite than Ki was, but he was near enough by now to see details. One of the six riders was gagged with a bandanna. The man's wrists were lashed to his saddlehorn, and his horse was being led by one of the other riders.

Ki could see only one reason why a bunch of hands would be escorting a bound and gagged man to the only big tree within twenty miles. He kicked his horse to a gallop.

In spite of his speed, the cowhands reached the tree first. Ki was still two hundred yards away when one of the Lazy G men began uncoiling his lariat. By the time Ki got within calling distance of the tree, the man holding the lariat had made a loop and dropped it over the neck of the helpless prisoner.

"Ho!" Ki shouted. "Stop what you are now doing!"

His words had the effect Ki hoped they would. The cowhands around the prisoner suspended their preparations for the hanging, and wheeled their horses to face Ki. He reined in when less than a dozen yards separated him from the stony-faced group. Though all the horses the cowpunchers rode bore the Lazy G brand, Ki found himself facing strangers.

"I do not need to ask what you men are planning to do," Ki said. He kept his voice low, pitched just high enough to carry to them. Long ago, Ki had observed that forcing a man to listen to a softly pitched voice drew his attention more effectively than did an angry shout.

3

"Who in hell are you, busting in like you got a right to stop us doing whatever we feel like?" one of the group snarled.

Ki looked closely at the men. He hadn't seen them on the Lazy G range before, but that wasn't unusual, for he and Jessie were often away from the Circle Star, and sometimes for long periods. Cowhands on the neighboring ranches as well as on the Starbuck spread had a common affliction: itchy feet. They came unannounced, worked until they'd earned enough money to carry them somewhere else, and moved on.

"I am the foreman of the Circle Star," Ki said. "You are on Starbuck land, so you will listen to me."

"Like hell we will! This sonofabitching rustler's going to be decorating that mesquite tree before he's five minutes older!"

Another of the cowhands, who'd been studying Ki's features, said, "Hey, you're some kind of greaser, but you damn sure ain't no Mex."

Ki ignored the remark. He looked from one to another of the five men, trying to read in their glowering faces how firmly they were committed to their purpose. At the same time, the Lazy G hands were studying him, trying to determine what kind of man he was. Ki's dress was just different enough from theirs to arouse their curiosity. He wore the same kind of faded jeans and the same kind of loosely fitting cotton twill shirt, and like all but one of them, Ki had on a vest over his shirt.

There the resemblance stopped. Ki's vest was leather, with creases and scuffed areas that denoted age and long use. Instead of the high-heeled, pointed-toed boots the Lazy G hands wore to a man, Ki's feet were shod in canvas slippers with rope soles. All the cowhands had on broad-brimmed Stetsons. Ki wore no hat, but had a sweat-stained cloth band tied around his head below his thick, glossy black hair. His slightly flattened nose and the epicanthic folds that gave an almond shape to his opaque black eyes betrayed his Japanese blood.

4

Ki waited until the Lazy G men had finished scrutinizing him before asking in the same low tone he'd used before, "Which of you is in charge?"

"We're all in charge, greaser," the man who'd spoken first replied contemptuously. "But seeing as Clem Petty called my name out first when he sent us to cut calves outta the nursery range, I guess I'm sorta the strawboss."

"Then order your companions to remove the noose from that man," Ki told him, nodding toward the prisoner. "Miss Starbuck would not wish to have a helpless person murdered on the Circle Star."

"Bullshit!" the strawboss snorted. "This ain't no murder, it's a execution!"

"That's handing it to him straight, Snag!" one of the Lazy G hands put in. "Don't take no lip from the greaser!"

"Hell, he ain't no greaser," another said. "He's some kind of a Chinee."

"By God, you're right, Ossie," the strawboss agreed.

Another of the Lazy G hands said, "Hell, he won't give us no trouble." His face twisted into an ugly grin. "I ain't seen a chink yet that was any good in a fight, lessen he had him a butcher knife or a cleaver. But I say we just don't pay him no mind, and finish what we come here to do."

"I'm with you, Fletch!" another of them seconded. "Go on, Snag. Tell him to get outta our way so we can get on with the rat-killing!"

When Snag did not speak at once, Ki broke the silence. He said calmly, "I now have three of your names to give to your foreman. I'm sure that Clem Petty would want all your names, so if you others would like to introduce yourselves—"

"Well, lah-di-dah!" Fletch broke in with an exaggerated simper. "This here chink talks just like a dude!"

"Claims he's gonna tell Clem on us, too," Snag said. "Now don't that scare you fellows?"

"It don't spook me, Snag," Ossie said. "How about you, Miller?"

"Oh, I'm about to pee my pants, I'm so scared," replied

5

the man whom Ossie had addressed. He turned to the cowhand who had not yet spoken. "Pete, we ain't heard from you. How about it?"

"Whatever you aim to do, count me in," the fifth man said.

From the corner of his eye, Ki saw an almost imperceptible movement of Snag's hand. He gave no sign that he noticed the strawboss, but gazed instead at the prisoner, whose eyes had been moving from one to another of his captors, but who could not speak because of the bandanna that gagged him.

"Perhaps if I knew why you are preparing to kill this man, I might not consider you murderers," Ki suggested. He still did not look at Snag, but kept his eyes on the prisoner.

"Now that ain't one goddamn bit of your business, chink," Stag retorted. "You're just going to shut up and set right where you are while we finish what we come here to do."

Snag swept his revolver from its holster as he spoke. Ki said nothing. He sat motionless, staring at the threatening muzzle of the strawboss's pistol.

When he finally spoke, Ki's voice was disarmingly gentle. He said, "You do not need to threaten me with your gun. You are five and I am one. And as you can see, I have neither rifle nor pistol."

Ki was careful not to say that he was weaponless, even though he was sure that the Lazy G men would have laughed at the simple devices he was carrying.

"By God, that's right," Pete said. "He ain't got a gun of no kind. Hell, Snag, we can do whatever we got a mind to. The Chinee won't give us no trouble."

Ossie spoke up. "Shit, Snag, we ain't gettin' noplace listening to this chink. He's a slick talker, I give you that, but let's do what we come here for and get it over with."

"Are you sure that is what you should do?" Ki asked Ossie. "By hanging that man"—he nodded toward the prisoner—"you make yourself into a murderer. Unless you can

6

prove to a judge that you were justified in killing him, prove that he is indeed a cattle thief, the law will hold you guilty."

Snag said quickly, "The law's got to catch us first to do that. And for all we know, you and that fellow over there's in cahoots. Both of you could be rustlers working together, the way you're sticking up for him."

"You're talking good sense now, Snag," Fletch said. "Maybe we better string him up with the young one. If we done that, we wouldn't have to worry about no witnesses."

"And what do you think Miss Starbuck would do if you were to kill one of her men?" Ki asked. "She would not forgive that, any more than she would overlook your trespassing on Starbuck land to hang a man who might be innocent."

"By God, Snag!" Miller said quickly, "I'd plumb forgot who this chink says he's working for! Now listen, I don't wanta get on the wrong side of anybody named Starbuck!"

"Me neither," Pete seconded. "What I've heard about that Starbuck woman, she can be a real hellion!"

"Hellion or not, we come here to hang a rustler," Snag told his companions. "Now let's do it and quit worrying about it! We know damn well we're right! No Starbuck nor nobody else is going to do nothing, after we're finished!"

Ki saw that he must play for time, and not just to let the tempers of the Lazy G hands cool down. He'd learned a psychological quirk that had saved him several times in the past. When a man who was not accustomed to gunplay drew a weapon, he was very conscious of its weight during the first few seconds it was in his hand. Then, as he became used to holding the gun, his muscles adjusted to its heft, and he would let the weapon wander off target.

"Well, chink?" the strawboss demanded. "You got anything else to say for yourself before we go ahead?"

"I have said nothing for myself, and will not speak of my own feelings," Ki replied in a totally unruffled voice. "I have spoken in behalf of this man you brought here to kill. I ask you again, why are you doing this?"

"Because the sneaking son of a bitch is a rustler!" Fletch

put in. "Damn it, Chinaman, if you're who you claim to be, you know damn well that when a rustler's caught he gets strung up from the closest tree!"

"I also know that rustlers work in gangs," Ki said. "There would have been a fight between you and a gang, if there were rustlers anywhere close by. I have been close to this place for quite some time and have not heard shooting."

"Well, we ain't been in no gunfight," Snag admitted. "But that don't change things one way or the other. We caught this snake sneaking around and he's getting what he deserves."

"Perhaps it is my stupidity which keeps me from understanding," Ki said apologetically. "But I am puzzled. A moment ago you said you knew your prisoner was a rustler. Now you tell me that you only caught him sneaking around."

"Ah, shit!" Ossie exploded. "All of us has been around ranches long enough to tell a rustler when we see one!"

"But how?" Ki asked again. "How can you say a man is a thief unless you have caught him stealing? Was this man driving some Lazy G cattle away?"

For a moment the cowhands exchanged glances, and then Snag said to Ki, "He didn't have no steers when we nabbed him. But we got all the proof we need that he's a rustler, all right."

"If you have proof, suppose you tell me what it is," Ki suggested. "So far you've said nothing that proves anything."

"All right!" Snag snapped. "Ossie, show this damn pesky Chinee what we found in that rustler's saddlebags."

Ossie turned around in his saddle, rummaged in the leather bags behind it for a moment, then came up with an iron rod about eighteen inches long. One end of the rod terminated in a short, tapered curve. The other end had been bent into a ring. Ossie held up the length of metal for Ki to look at.

Ki had recognized the metal object at once. It was called a "running iron" by the cowhands, because with a little skillful manipulation by an expert, the burned-in lines of a brand on a steer's hindquarters could be run together to change the brand's meaning.

The letters *O* or *C* could be transformed into the numbers *8* or *6* or *9*, and *C* could also be made into *O* or *G*; *7* into *9* or *4*; *D* or *P* could be altered to become *B*; *V* turned into *N, M,* or *W;* or a symbol could be added to turn a letter brand into a letter with a slash, line, or circle. There were any number of changes that an expert running-iron user could create.

Brands were often changed when cattle were sold, but almost equally often, a new brand was simply added beside the old one. In an economy based on cattle, brands were generally the only identification steers had, the only way by which their ownership could be established. All ranches registered their brands at the nearest county seat, and the county authorities saw to it that a record of the brand was forwarded to the state territorial capital, where all brands were also registered.

"Well?" Snag asked Ki. "You satisfied now? If you're the foreman of the Circle Star, you know damn well that here in Texas it's against the law to even *carry* a running iron."

Ki nodded thoughtfully. He knew that the law cited by Snag did indeed exist; mere possession of a running iron drew a minimum sentence of five years in prison for the man having it. However, he'd been watching the prisoner's face while he and the Lazy G crew talked, and the pleading he'd seen in the man's eyes could not be ignored. Ki knew the look of guilt, open as well as disguised, and his sixth sense told him that the eyes he'd looked into were not those of a guilty man.

"What you say about the law is true," Ki admitted, watching Snag without letting his attention be noticed. "But it does not automatically make a rustler of every man who has a running iron. Even if it did, the man must be brought before a judge and a jury and be legally tried and convicted.

It is not the same thing as catching a rustler in the act of stealing cattle."

"Aw, to hell with that shit!" Fletch growled. "We ain't got time to fool around with the law! It's too damn slow!"

"But it is the law," Ki pointed out gently.

"Look here, chink, we got as much respect for the law as you have!" Miller said. "Except it's like Fletch just told you, it takes too long. We'd lose two days taking this rustler to the county seat. We'd have to stay there a day or two while he was being tried, then it'd take us another two days to get back! We got work to do!"

Ki asked in his softest voice, "Tell me, Miller, would you feel the same way if you were sitting there with a noose around your neck, waiting to be hanged?"

"Now what the hell kinda question is that?" Miller asked.

"A fair one," Ki replied.

"Damned if it is!" Fletch snorted. He turned to Snag. "Well? How about it, Snag? Has everybody got cold feet, or are we going to string up this worthless cattle-rustling bastard?"

"If you still feel like doing it, we will," Snag said. He looked from one to another of the Lazy G men. Fletch nodded at once, so did Miller. Ossie inclined his head after a moment of hesitation.

Pete said, "I was about to change my mind, but if the rest of you're set on going ahead, count me in."

"That's settled, then," Snag told them. He went on, "You already got your rope on him, Fletch. Take the slack outta the noose and toss the other end over that mesquite limb."

Fletch toed his horse up beside the prisoner, whose eyes had grown increasingly fearful as he watched and listened to the discussion that was to decide his fate. The Lazy G man pulled the noose tight and tossed the free end of the rope over the one branch of the mesquite that was sturdy enough to hold a man's weight. He was starting back to join the others when Snag spoke.

"Damn it, get his hands untied from his saddlehorn! If

10

they're still fastened, the rope won't pull him off the horse! Ain't you never strung up a rustler before, Fletch?"

With an angry look at the strawboss, Fletch untied the pigging-string that secured the prisoner's hands to his saddlehorn. While he was still pulling the knot of the pigging-string when retying the man's hands, the victim struck.

★

Chapter 2

With his hands bound, the accused prisoner had no weapon except his head. As Fletch was raising his head after examining the pigging-string to make sure the knot was tightly cinched, the prisoner arched his back and butted Fletch in the jaw. The unexpected impact almost sent the Lazy G man from his saddle, and the prisoner kicked frantically at his horse's flanks, trying to get the animal to move. Belatedly the horse started off, but with no guiding hands on its reins, it ran directly toward the other men from the Lazy G.

Ossie, Miller, and Pete closed in around the hapless prisoner and grabbed his arms. Fletch spurred up to join them. Snag did not move to help them, but kept his attention on Ki. During their long discussion, Snag had allowed the muzzle of his revolver to sag, as Ki had expected he would, but now he brought it up to threaten Ki once more. He did not give Ki his full attention, but darted his eyes away from time to time, watching his men lash the prisoner's arms behind his back, tighten the noose of the lariat, and toss its end over the limb again.

Ki had been waiting for an opportunity to create just such a diversion without getting shot himself. He used the moments when Snag's attention was distracted to drop one hand to his waist and free the loose knot that held in place the *surushin* he wore instead of a belt. By the time Snag's eyes were on him again, Ki was once more sitting motionless.

"You decided to give in, Chinaman?" Snag asked mockingly.

13

"I have decided to see how far you will let your men go," Ki replied.

"Don't make no mistake, they'll go all the way," Snag told Ki. "And after that rustler bastard's kicked his last kick, them and me's going to make up our minds what to do with you."

"I've done you no harm yet," Ki pointed out.

"Right enough. But it ain't in the cards to let you go free after you seen us give that rustler what he's got coming. Only thing we got to settle is whether to use the rope or a gun."

Ki did not answer, but turned his eyes pointedly to the scene under the mesquite. There, Fletch, Miller, Ossie, and Pete were having a low-voiced discussion, apparently over the part each of them was to play in the lynching.

Whatever the subject of the discussion, it was soon over. While Fletch and Pete stationed themselves on each side of the prisoner, Miller knotted the free end of the lariat that had become a lynching rope around his saddlehorn. Ossie led Miller's horse in a small half-circle away from the tree, backing it until the slack had been removed from the rope. The lariat now stretched tautly from the bound man's neck, over the limb to Miller's saddlehorn.

Miller nodded to Fletch and Pete. They each raised one hand in the air. Ki glanced at Snag, and saw that his eyes were fixed on the victim. Fletch and Pete brought their hands down in hard slaps on the rump of the prisoner's horse. The horse leaped forward and the lariat hummed as it tightened.

Ki whipped out the *surushin*, whirled it twice around his head, and launched it at Snag. The rope sang through the air, pulled taut by the lead weights at either end, and wrapped itself around Snag, securing his gun hand to his body. In one fluid movement that was a continuation of throwing the *surushin*, Ki reached into one of the many pockets of his leather vest, then extended his arm in a rapid whiplash motion. A razor-edged *shuriken* throwing-star left his hand and spun, glittering, through the air. The small,

14

star-shaped disc sank itself into the mesquite limb where the hanging rope was drawn tight over it, severing the lariat cleanly. The prisoner dropped to the ground.

For a moment the angry cowhands did not grasp what had happened. Then they identified Ki as the one who had thwarted them, and, as one man, spurred toward him.

Ki covered most of the distance that separated him from Pete and Fletch while the two Lazy G hands were still gaping at the sight of their prisoner's horse galloping away.

Pete's hand was sliding up to the butt of his revolver as Ki closed in. Before he had the gun started from its holster, Ki linked his own arm through the crook of Pete's elbow. While his horse was carrying him past his adversary, Ki locked his sinewy hand on the Lazy G man's wrist.

Using his biceps and Pete's own ribcage as lever and fulcrum, he brought Pete's right arm up and away from his body, then twisted the arm up and back until, with a sharp, popping snap, the bone of Pete's upper arm came out of its socket at the shoulder.

Screaming with pain, Pete dropped off his horse and lay writhing on the ground. His dislocated right arm flopped in response to the jerking of his body, the arm itself now beyond any of the man's efforts to control its movements.

Ki's rush had carried him beyond Fletch, who now had to turn his mount in order to bring his gun to bear. Ki yanked at the reins of his combat-wise horse. The animal planted its hooves and spun in its own length, leaving Fletch still pointing his pistol at the empty space where the Lazy G man thought Ki's horse would have taken him.

Out of the corner of his eye, Ki saw that Miller and Ossie had now drawn their revolvers. A quick glance behind him confirmed that he'd put himself between them and Fletch. Neither Miller nor Ossie could fire at Ki without the risk of hitting Fletch. For the moment they were forced to sit and watch, holding their useless guns.

Ki's mount completed its turn and he kicked the animal ahead toward Fletch. He reached his objective just as Fletch's horse, turning in response to its rider's frantic tugs on the reins, brought Fletch's body squarely in line with Ki. Ki was now less than an arm's length away. Fletch started bringing up his gun.

Ki thrust his forearm out to stop Fletch's arm from rising. His stiffened fingers slid along Fletch's arm and stabbed into the Lazy G man's diaphragm. Ki's stone-hard fingertips smashed into Fletch's solar plexus. The shock of the thrust carried with paralyzing force through the shallow wall of flesh between the ribs and stomach muscles, and into the complex of nerves that lay just below the breastbone.

Fletch's face twisted into an agonized grimace as the paralysis sped from the nerve-center and stopped him from breathing. His shoulders tensed as they arched backward, and his revolver dropped from nerveless fingers. For a moment Fletch poised in his saddle, unnaturally erect, then slumped and slid slowly to the ground, one booted foot caught in his stirrup.

As Fletch fell, Ki rolled out of his own saddle, knowing that Ossie and Miller would have a clear shot at him, and that they would not hesitate to use their guns. They were already spurring toward the jammed-up animals when Ki left his saddle. He waited, sheltered between the two horses. Ossie came abreast of Ki's horse, Ki dove between the animal's legs and rose to his knees as Ossie's horse came abreast.

Reaching up, Ki grasped Ossie's ankle and pulled the booted foot out of the stirrup. Yanking Ossie's leg straight, Ki put his shoulder under the calf and reared up. Ossie let his pistol fall when he began flailing his arms, trying to stay in his saddle. Ki brought the leg up higher. Shoving the booted foot toward Ossie, Ki clamped his free hand on the man's knee. He pulled down on the knee while pushing up on the ankle, then twisted both hands sharply, to dislocate Ossie's hip. Ossie tumbled from his saddle, thudded to the earth, and lay still, moaning.

Snag was still fighting to free himself from the entangling ends of the *surushin*, but Miller had circled halfway around the three milling horses and was trying to get a shot off at Ki. The horses were in the way, and Miller reined his mount around to get Ki in his sights.

Ki moved the instant the horse started to turn. Squirming under Ossie's horse, Ki vaulted up on the rump of Miller's horse while the man's back was turned. Perched precariously behind Miller, Ki smashed the steel-hard edge of his right hand down on the sparsely fleshed tendons that ran from neck to shoulder. His chop tore loose the tendons and the nerves anchored to them.

Stiffening in his saddle, Miller's eyes rolled upward and he toppled to the ground, his body board-stiff.

Ki slid off the horse's rump. His own mount had worked free of the mill now, and was only a long step away. Ki leaped into its saddle and started back toward Snag.

During the few seconds Ki had needed to dispose of the four Lazy G hands, the strawboss had stayed bound by the *surushin*'s horsehair rope. The twirling lead balls on each end of the flexible rope had met and wound together behind Snag's back. His right hand, still holding his gun, was pinned firmly to his chest, the muzzle of the weapon pointing up into the empty sky.

Snag began spewing out obscenities as he saw Ki coming close to him. He stopped trying to reach the entwined ends of the *surushin* with his left hand and tried to reach it up and take the revolver from his right. Ki reached him before Snag could make the exchange. Without drawing rein, Ki stiffened the fingers of his right hand once more and drove his fingertips into Snag's exposed larnyx. The obscenities choked off into a muffled, gasping wheeze as Snag fought vainly for both speech and breath.

Ki lifted the man's pistol from his weakening hand and tossed the gun as far as he could. He stayed close to Snag only long enough to release the *surushin*, and freed it just as the strawboss fell to the ground, his chest heaving as he struggled to fill his lungs.

Less than a minute had passed since Ki launched his

17

attack on the Lazy G crew. Ahead, he saw the prisoner. The man's arms were still bound behind his back. From his neck, the rope severed by the *shuriken* trailed on the dry earth. Ki nudged his horse into a gallop and caught up.

"I still don't know whether I was right in saving your neck from that lynching rope," Ki remarked, unwrapping the pigging-string from the man's wrists. As he began to work at the knot in the bandanna that still gagged the prisoner's mouth, he went on, "But as soon as you can talk, I'll listen to your side of the story and make up my mind whether to let you go or turn you over to the sheriff." Ki whipped the bandanna free, and for the first time got a close-up look at the prisoner's grime-streaked face. He stared and said unbelievingly, "Why, you're—you're just a young boy!"

"I'm old enough to take care of myself," the youth retorted hoarsely, through dry, cracked lips.

Ki took his canteen from the looped saddlestring that held it, and passed it to the young man. He said, "You'll talk easier after you've had some water."

While the youth was drinking, Ki sized him up. He was not more than eighteen, and was likely even younger, but his build was husky. His face was unlined under its coating of dirt, and the sparse stubble that showed through the dust and grime indicated that he'd only been shaving for a couple of years at most. His lips and chin were firm, with just a suggestion of grim purpose in their lines. His bare head was covered with a thick shock of light brown hair that badly needed combing.

A long gurgling drink and a second, slower sip of the water freed the youth's throat. "I sure owe you a lot, mister," he told Ki. "I'd've been dead and swinging on that tree to dry if you hadn't come along when you did."

"Save your thanks," Ki advised him. "First I want to know your name and where you're from."

"Charley..." the youth hesitated and then finished in a rush of words, "Smith. And I'm from over in central Texas."

18

Ki wasn't taken in by the obviously false name, but he decided to let both that and the evasion as to the exact location of the young man's home pass for the moment.

"Well, Charley Smith," he began, "you might not want to answer my next question, and you might try to lie your way out of the scrape you got into, but I want to know why you were carrying a running iron. Don't you know there's a law against it?"

"I sure do, *now*," Smith replied. "But I didn't till you and them other fellows got to talking about it."

"You'll have to do better than that," Ki warned him.

"Look, mister, I can't do better'n the truth, and the truth is that I found that damned piece of iron someplace between the Box B ranch house and the Lazy G. I don't know exactly whose range it was on, but I can sure take you back there and you can see the print it made in the dirt where it was laying."

"All right, we'll let the running iron pass for a minute," Ki told Smith. "What were you doing crossing the Box B?"

"I work there. For Mr. Brad Close. I did until yesterday, that is. Then..."

"Well, go on. What happened yesterday?"

Smith hesitated, his unlined brow knotting into a frown. After a moment he said curtly, "I got fired."

"Why?"

"Because after we'd finished rounding up what cattle was left after them rustlers took Mr. Close's market herd, the foreman said there wasn't going to be enough work on the ranch so's they'd need me any longer."

Ki was as quick to discern the truth as he was to smell a lie, and young Smith's explanation rang true. He asked, "How long ago was the Box B market herd rustled?"

"Let's see..." Smith thought briefly and said, "A little bit more'n two weeks ago."

That would explain why he and Jessie hadn't heard about it when they'd returned to the Starbuck ranch, Ki thought. In only two weeks, the news wouldn't have spread beyond the Box B. He put another question to Smith. "You didn't get into some sort of trouble that made the Box B foreman fire you?" Then quickly he asked, "What's his name, by the way?"

"His name's Dave Martin," Smith replied promptly. "And I didn't get crossways of him nor of Mr. Close, neither. What Dave said was that I was just hired on as an extra hand to help drive the market herd to the shipping pens, and being the last man they'd put on, I had to be the first one they let go."

This reply, too, rang true. Ki said, "I don't suppose you'd object to riding back to the Box B with me, then?"

"I wouldn't mind one bit."

Ki nodded. "I guess that's all I need to know," he said. Come on. We'll be on our way."

"What about them men that was setting out to hang me?"

"They won't be chasing us, if that's what's worrying you."

Twisting in his saddle, young Smith looked back toward the mesquite tree. He said, "It looks to me like they're still laying on the ground."

Ki didn't bother to turn his head, but said mildly, "I imagine they are. They won't be after you again."

"What in the dickens did you do to them?"

"It'd take too long to explain," Ki smiled. "Just take my word that they won't be after you."

Ki nudged his horse into motion and Charley Smith did the same. They'd ridden side by side for only a short distance when Smith suddenly reined in.

"Wait a minute," he told Ki. "This ain't the way to the Box B. It's in the other direction."

"Of course it is. And you can call me Ki, by the way."

"But I thought you said we were going—"

Ki corrected him. "I didn't say where we were going. I asked you if you'd mind going back to the Box B, and you told me you wouldn't. When you said that, I knew you'd told me the truth."

"I don't see how you could be sure."

"Very simple, Charley Smith. You knew Dave Martin and Brad Close would back up your story. If you'd been lying, you'd have objected to going back."

"What about the running iron I was carrying?"

"I used the same test of reason. You offered to show me where you picked it up. You know the ground had a mark where the iron had been lying, for quite some time, I imagine. So that part of your story was truthful too."

"You figure things out pretty good, mister."

"Ki is my name, Charley. I told you to use it."

"Ki, then. And you're really the foreman of the Circle Star?"

"That's where we're going now. Would I be taking you there if I were lying?"

"No. No, I guess not."

They rode on for a short distance in silence before Ki asked Charley, "How badly did the rustlers strip the Box B?"

"Pretty bad, I guess. Mr. Close took some of the men and tried to trail 'em, but they came back next day. He said the rustlers was heading for the Rio Grande, that they'd got such a big start they'd have his steers in Mexico before him and the men could catch up to 'em."

"Yes, Brad would know. He's good at reading trail sign."

Charley frowned. "He said something about the Laredo Loop, Ki. Everybody but me seemed to know what he meant, and I was sorta shy about asking, even if I didn't know."

Briefly, Ki explained to the young greenhorn that Laredo was the main shipping point for the ranches that lay within easy trail-driving distance of its railroad line. He went on to describe the way rustlers along the Rio Grande operated, stealing herds in Texas and getting them across the river into Mexico as quickly as possible.

Once out of reach of U.S. law, the rustlers could alter the cattle brands whenever it suited them. Then they drove the herds in a loop through Mexican territory, moving away from the river to the railroad shipping-pens at Laredo. They had no trouble selling them there; plenty of cattle buyers were happy to pay the reduced prices that steers brought on the west side of the Rio Grande without asking too many questions about the origin of the herd.

"So that's where the name 'Laredo Loop' got started?" Charley asked after hearing Ki's explanation.

"That's it. From what I understand, it's been going on since there have been ranches in Texas and outlaws in Mexico who are ready to steal their cattle. I'd guess the running iron that almost got you lynched was dropped by some of the gang that stole the Box B herd."

"Well, if I ever see another one lying around, I'll sure know better than to pick it up." Charley looked around and said suddenly, "I never did ask you where we're heading, Ki, after you told me why we wasn't going back to the Box B."

"To the Circle Star, of course. I'm not sure just how many hands we've got, or whether we need any more right now, but Ed Wright or Speedy—that's Ed's top hand— might hire on another cowpoke."

"If you're the Circle Star foreman, how come you don't know something like that?"

"I'm not the kind of foreman that Dave Martin is at the Box B, Charley," Ki explained. "I'm more of a manager. Part of my job is going with Miss Jessica Starbuck when she travels, so I'm not at the ranch all the time."

"I've heard a lot about the Circle Star," young Smith said. "And about Miss Starbuck and her daddy. I never did hear about you, though. Is Ki all the name you've got?"

"It is all the name I use." A tinge of bitterness crept into Ki's voice. "I lost my name in my own country." He shrugged and added, "It does not really matter to me, any more than your own real name seems to matter to you."

Smith stared at Ki. "How did you figure that out?"

"You've given yourself away several times, Charley."

"Well, if you really want to know—"

Ki quickly raised his hand and shook his head. "No. I don't want to share your secrets. My guess is that you've run away from home because your parents picked a trade they expected you to follow, and you wanted only to be a cowhand."

"I still do, Ki. That's all I ever wanted to be."

"Then a cowhand is what you should be. But even if you haven't asked for it, I'll give you a bit of advice."

"What's that?"

"Sometime soon, write your parents and tell them you're well. And perhaps you can say you're happy, if there's a job for you on the Circle Star."

"Well . . ." Charley Smith hesitated, then nodded. "I don't guess it'd hurt me none to do that."

"Good. And we'll find out about the job soon. In another ten or fifteen miles, we'll be in sight of the Circle Star."

They rode on in silence then, as the sun dropped to afternoon, until the buildings of the Starbuck ranch became visible on the horizon.

★

Chapter 3

Left to herself after Ki's departure, Jessie strolled idly around the sprawling main house to the horse corral. Sun, the magnificent palomino stallion that was her favorite mount, came prancing up to greet her. Jessie rubbed the golden animal's velvet nose, and whispered into his ear how happy she was to be with him again. Neighing, Sun tossed his head, reared up on his hind legs, and moved with careful balance toward the corral gate.

"Reckon he's right glad to see you, Miss Jessie," the horse wrangler said as he came from the hay shed to investigate the reason for the palomino's neighs. "He's in pretty good shape for not working such a long time, ain't he?"

"He looks just fine, Speedy," Jessie replied. She gazed across the range land that stretched invitingly from the corral's bars, and said, "Saddle him for me, will you, while I go inside and change? I think I need a little ride as much as Sun does."

She got back just as Speedy tightened the last cinch-straps of the saddle he'd put on the palomino's back. At the ranch, Jessie defied the convention of sidesaddles and rode astride. She'd donned her jeans, skin-tight, with tapered legs that fitted into her ornately stitched high-heeled boots. She'd also put on her pistol belt, with the customized Colt that had been one of her father's gifts nestled in its holster. Waving away Speedy's cupped hands, she swung into the saddle, and, with a toss of his head, the palomino started for the open range.

Sun had rested longer than usual during Jessie's absence from the ranch. The big palomino pawed the hard earth and whuffled, as though to remind his mistress that he had a lot of unused running stored up in his muscular legs.

Jessie took the hint. She turned the stallion away from the ranch house, and after walking him far enough to get the stiffness out of his legs, she let the reins go slack and leaned forward to slap lightly on his withers.

Sun responded at once. Mighty muscles rippling under his tawny hide, he burst into a gallop. Feeling the fresh warm breeze on her face, Jessie reached up and pushed off her brown Stetson, letting it fall back on her shoulders, held only by the thong under her chin. She shook her head to free her hair; it streamed behind her in ripples of tawny gold, a shade darker and a bit more copper-hued than the flowing blond mane and tail of the speeding palomino.

When she judged that Sun had worked off enough of his energy for the moment, Jessie pulled lightly on the reins. The big horse shook his head as though to protest the command, but slowed obediently. Jessie straightened up in her saddle, a contented smile parting her full red lips. Then, through the thin haze of tears the warm breeze had brought into her eyes, she saw a rider ahead, and the smile gave way to a thoughtful frown.

A short distance away, a little draw offered a place of partial concealment for a horse and rider. Jessie guided the high-stepping palomino to the shallow gully and reined in. Sun tossed his head when he felt the pull of the reins. Like his mistress, the great golden stallion chafed at restraint; he was still bursting with pent-up energy.

"Stand, Sun," Jessica told the horse softly. "Let's wait and see who's coming up on us before we go any farther."

Frowning into the sun, her emerald-green eyes drawn into slits, she tried to identify the rider. The sunlight in her eyes baffled recognition. Jessie could be sure of only one thing: The man riding toward her wasn't a Circle Star hand, or she'd have recognized him when she first sighted him.

Wisdom born of sorrow still remembered had told Jessie

26

to be careful when she saw the rider approaching. She'd learned one bitter lesson from her father's murder: No one who bore the Starbuck name could count on being safe from attack, even in the middle of the small kingdom that was formed by the sprawling Circle Star Ranch.

Instinct brought Jessie's fingers to the cool grips of the custom-made Colt .38/.44 in its tooled holster at her side as she watched the horseman draw closer. Then she relaxed and toed Sun's flank, sending him scrambling up the sloping wall of the *barranca* to greet the old friend and neighbor she'd at last recognized.

"Howdy, Jessica," Bradford Close called to her as Sun brought Jessie near enough for his voice to reach her. "Didn't look to meet up with you this far from the house, but I'm glad I did. I was just on my way to visit you."

"It's nice of you to think about stopping by, Brad," Jessie replied. "How's everything at the Box B?"

"I guess it's still there, Jessie, but I ain't sure of much of anything right now."

Jessie sensed trouble behind Close's reply. She asked, "You haven't been home for a while, then?"

"No. I been on a little trip and figured to swing over to see you before I went home. I don't guess much could've happened to the place, though. I ain't really been gone long, even if it seems to me like I have."

Close reined in at the rim of the *barranca,* and Jessie clucked, sending Sun up the shallow side to join him. She took in her neighbor's appearance at a glance. Brad Close seemed to have aged ten years since she'd seen him last, though that had been only two or three months earlier. Now his face showed lines that had not been visible the last time she'd talked with him. His clothing seemed to hang on him instead of fitting snugly, and the spark that had always lurked in his ice-blue eyes had been extinguished.

Glancing at Close's horse, her expert eye noted the animal's ribs outlined under its hide, and the twitching of its hind-leg muscles, signs of many days of rough travel.

"You must have had a hard trip," Jessica said. "Let's

27

ride on to the house together, it's only a few miles. You'll stay for supper and the night, of course."

"No, Jessica. I thank you for asking me, but I've got to get on home. I wasn't aiming to stop long, just a few minutes to rest my horse and have a little visit with you. We can talk all we need to here, and then I'll ride on to my place."

"I'm not going to take no for an answer, Brad," she told him firmly. "I don't know how long you've been in the saddle, but it's time you got out of it and rested."

Close's fingers were busy rolling a cigarette, and Jessie noticed that his fingers were trembling. She said nothing. He licked the thin paper cylinder to seal its edges, then touched a match to it and blew a thin stream of blue smoke before he replied.

Slowly, nodding as he spoke, the Box B owner said, "Maybe stopping over ain't such a bad idea at that, Jessie. Seems like I use up what little zip I got left sooner than I used to."

"Unless you'd rather stay here and rest a few minutes, we can start for the ranch right now," she suggested.

"Let's just do that. You're right about me having a hard trip. I was down south of the border, and the news I'm coming back home with ain't good. Then I got to thinking about what your daddy used to say—that bad news ain't as bad when you got a friend to tell it to—so I swung over this way."

"I'm glad you did. Father always valued your friendship, and I know you two spent quite a lot of time together before . . ." Jessie stopped, seeking to avoid the words that had been on the tip of her tongue, and finally concluded, "When he was here at the ranch."

"Yes. And I miss that man mortally, Jessica!" Then Close added hurriedly, "Not the way you miss him, of course, but in my own way."

"We all miss him in our own way," Jessie said. She paused for a moment, waiting for Close to begin. She could tell that he needed help, but was too proud to ask outright. She went on, "Why don't you save your bad news until we get to the house and you've had a drink. We've still got a lot of that whiskey you and Father liked so much."

"Now that's the best offer I've had all day. We won't be able to move fast, though. This old hoss is tireder than me."

"You'd better take one of ours to go the rest of the way, then. Leave yours, and Speedy will have him back in good shape when you've got time to pick him up."

Jessie and Close talked little during the rest of the short ride to the ranch. She waited until Close had washed up and they were sitting in the big central room of the main house. Only after the old rancher had swallowed one good drink of the smooth, aged bourbon she poured him, and she'd refilled his glass, did Jessie bring the conversation back to his problems.

She said, "If you'd like to tell me your bad news, Brad, I'm listening."

"Well, it's not anything new."

"Father used to say there were only two things that bothered a Texas rancher, drought and rustlers." Jessie smiled, but her face grew serious instantly and she said, "I know we've had enough rain this spring. Who's been stealing your cattle, Brad?"

"If I knew, I wouldn't be here talking to you now, Jessica." Brad Close's mouth snapped into a thin, angry line. "I'm just riding back from all the way down to the Rio Grande and beyond. Somebody stole my market herd."

Jessie knew what that meant. On a spread the size of the Box B, a market herd would include virtually every salable steer that could be rounded up. A loss like that could cripple even a big ranch, and the Box B wasn't in that category.

Her voice showing her concern, she asked, "All of it?"

"Every single last steer. Heads, horns, hides, and tails," Close said grimly.

"How long had the herd been gone before you found it'd been rustled?"

"I don't rightly know, Jessie. A week, week and a half. I was sorta resting the steers before I started the drive to

29

the shipping pens. They was on that fenced half section on the south of my spread, and you'd remember that's a good four miles from the main house. I wasn't worried about the critters, so I didn't set a night herder. Me and the hands was out making one last gather before we drove to market, so it was a while before anybody went there."

Jessie saw that Close was at the point of collapse from exhaustion and worry. She said carefully, "I don't want to offend you, Brad, but you're tired out. Why don't you go up to one of the guest rooms and have a nap? Ki will be back before supper, and after we've eaten we can sit down and talk things over. Maybe among the three of us, we can figure something out."

Close started to protest, but a bout of yawning overpowered him. He nodded and said reluctantly, "I reckon that's the sensible thing to do, Jessie. I'll feel better after I catch forty winks. I guess I just ain't had enough sleep to do me, the last couple of weeks."

With Close settled into one of the upstairs guest rooms, Jessie stepped out on the veranda of the big house. She paced restlessly, went back into the house and to the kitchen for a cup of coffee, and returned to the veranda, where she was sitting when Ki and Charley Smith rode up. Ki reined in, and young Smith followed suit.

Ki introduced Smith to Jessie, then told the youth, "The horse corral's just past the hay shed, over there. I don't suppose you'll mind leading my horse when you go. Speedy'll tell you what to do. Then go on to the bunkhouse and find Ed Wright. If he's not in off the range yet, wait for him. Tell him I've promised you meals and a bunk for a few days, and a job if he's got one. You'll find out fast enough if we can hire you on."

After Smith was out of earshot, Jessie asked Ki, "Where did you find him? Was he lost out on the range?"

Ki quickly related the afternoon's happenings, winding up by saying, "So, I brought Smith back with me, to see if there might be a job for him here."

"Which you knew there would be, of course."

"Of course," Ki agreed. "A month's work, at least, so the boy will have traveling money if we don't keep him."

Jessie smiled. "Another orphan, Ki. How many does this one make that you've brought here just for a little while?"

"Enough, I suppose. But remember, Jessie, I was a stray like Charley Smith when your father took me in."

"Yes. But there'll never be another one like you, Ki. I can't blame you for keeping on trying, though."

They started into the house. Ki said, "Smith told me about the situation at the Box B. It worries me. Brad Close's market herd was stolen—"

"I know," Jessie interrupted. "Brad's upstairs right now, sleeping. He was so exhausted—"

"You know about the rustlers, then." When Jessie nodded, Ki went on, "Those gangs work in a pattern, remember. The chances are they'll hit us or the Lazy G next."

"After what you told me about your run-in this afternoon, the Lazy G's going to be shorthanded," Jessie frowned. "They'd be an easy target. I suppose we would too, unless we put out night herders. But the Lazy G's a syndicate ranch, and they'd have the resources to tide them over. We could recover too, if we lost a herd. Not that I'd want to."

"I'll talk to Ed tomorrow," Ki said. "Charley Smith might be luckier here than he was at the Box B."

Jessie was still pursuing her original train of thought. She went on, "Brad didn't say so outright, Ki, but I got the idea that losing his market herd could just about wipe him out. And he's been a good friend since my father's time."

"You'll help him, of course?"

"Of course. Maybe a loan from one of the Starbuck banks to tide him over while he's rebuilding his herds. He wouldn't let us help him directly, I know, but he wouldn't realize we'd have anything to do with a loan from a bank."

"We'll see how he feels after supper," Ki said. "And it's time for me to get cleaned up. I'll be down in time to eat."

Rested and refreshed by a good dinner, Close was better able to give a complete account of what had happened when he set out to trail his stolen cattle as he, Jessie, and Ki sat

31

in the big main room of the ranch house after they'd eaten.

"I didn't waste no time," the old rancher said. "Took out after 'em before the trail got any colder."

"Alone?" Ki asked.

"Sure. Hell, Ki, I wasn't looking for a fight. I was out to find out where my steers was. If I'd been lucky enough to run that bunch to their hideout, I'd've got a bunch together to give them rustlers a real bellyful. There's always men with guns for hire south of the river."

"But you didn't find the hideout?" Jessie asked.

"Nope. Oh, it was easy enough to trail the herd from the Box B to the river, and I found where they crossed, and followed the trail partway into Mexico."

"Only partway? You're not the kind of man to give up on a trail like that, Brad," Jessie observed, frowning. "What happened?"

"What happened was that whoever was bossing them rustlers had sense enough to leave four or five men as a rear guard. I had to dodge that bunch over half of Coahuila before I shook 'em off my trail."

"And the main bunch got away with your cattle, of course?"

"You bet they did! You know what the country's like on the other side of the Rio Grande, south of the Big Bend."

"Yes. Pretty much what it's like on this side. Baked earth that doesn't hold tracks well, rough desert mile after mile, and no real landmarks to go by."

Close nodded. "You've named it, Jessica. Oh, I never did get what you'd call lost. After I shook off the rustlers' rear guards, I swung north by way of San Pedro, and stopped to talk to the *rurales* that's headquartered there. But all I got from 'em was what the little boy shot at."

"Meaning nothing?" Ki asked.

"Meaning nothing," Brad agreed. "They wasn't about to put theirselves out for a gringo. Well, I could understand that, so after I got back on this side of the Rio Grande, I angled up to Fort Chaplin to tell our own soldiers what was going on."

Jessie took advantage of the pause to ask, "They weren't any more help than the *rurales* had been?"

"Maybe not even as much."

"I can't understand that," she said. "Captain Stanford has always tried to do what he could to help the ranchers when bandits from the other side of the river give us trouble."

"Stanford's been transferred," Close said. "They sent a young pipsqueak Yankee from back East to take his place."

"Surely some of the men who were serving under Captain Stanford are still there, though," Ki put in.

"Oh, sure. But they can't lift a finger to help a body if the fort commander don't tell 'em to."

"And the new commander wouldn't?"

"Not for a minute!" Close stopped long enough to take a swallow of coffee. He went on, "Hell, that new man never even caught on to what I was talking about when I told him I figured the old Laredo Loop was working again."

Jessie shook her head. "I just can't imagine the army doing nothing when we ask for help."

"I guess the old army's changing, Jessica," Close said. "You take this young Lieutenant Farnam that's taken Stanford's place, now. He wasn't no brighter'n Adam's off-ox when it come to him understanding what I tried to tell him."

Somewhere deep in Jessie's mind, a tiny warning bell tinkled when she heard the lieutenant's name. She asked, "Farnam? What's his first name, Brad?"

"Joe, which I'd guess is short for Joseph."

"Did he happen to mention where he'd come from?"

"One of them big old towns back East. Boston, I believe it was. Why?"

"Oh, just an idea I had. Farnam isn't a very common name."

"You mean you might know him, or his kinfolks?"

Jessie shook her head. "No. Except that the name sounded familiar for a moment. But it's not important, Brad. Go on with your story."

"Well, there ain't much more to tell, Jessica. This little

puffed-up lieutenant's got no more idea of what them soldiers he bosses is supposed to do than that palomino of yours would have. I wanted him to get some patrols out along the river and try to nab a bunch of them rustlers with a herd of steers they'd stole, before they could get over on the other side of the river and change brands on 'em. No, he says, he can't do that, the army's got orders now not to mix up in civilian business. Go see the sheriff, he told me."

"I'm sure you explained to him that the sheriff's at the county seat, which is a three-day ride from the river?"

"Sure I did. He said he was sorry, but that's all the satisfaction I got. Now if your daddy was still here—" Close stopped short and shook his head. "I guess I didn't have no call to say that, Jessica. I'm sorry."

"You shouldn't be, Brad. I agree with you, if Father were here, he'd get some hands from the Box B and the Lazy G and some from our place, and put an end to the rustling. But..." her voice trailed off.

Soberly, Close said, "Yeah." He yawned again. "Well, I've told you about all I know. And if you'll excuse me, I think I'll go back upstairs and catch up on the rest of that sleep I lost."

"And bed sounds good to me," Ki said, standing up.

"I know you're both tired," Jessie told them. "We'll talk some more at breakfast, when we're fresh. Among the three of us, we ought to be able to think of some way to stop this new Laredo Loop gang before it does any more damage. Then we can sleep peacefully all night, every night."

★

Chapter 4

After Ki and Brad Close had gone upstairs, Jessie sat alone in the big main room, sipping the last swallows of her coffee. Slowly the house grew quiet as the noises from above—doors opening and closing, soft footsteps in the hall—died away as Ki and Close settled down in their own bedrooms.

Poor Brad! she thought to herself. *Losing a herd that could mean the difference between keeping his spread and having to close it out. And being given such rude treatment by the army must have been the last straw. Which reminds me—*

Jessie stood up and went into the big square room that had been Alex Starbuck's office and den. She sat down in the oversized leather chair in front of the huge oak rolltop desk that had been her father's. Alex had bought the desk when he began his first business venture in San Francisco, a small importing firm dealing in goods from the Orient.

At that time the Circle Star had been a small specialized spread, breeding fine horses as a sideline to catching the wild mustangs that roamed the prairie, breaking them and training them as cattle ponies. The first expansion of his interests had been almost accidental. To tide the Circle Star over a long period of drought that had brought ranching to a standstill, Starbuck had taken a shipload of fine horses to the Far East. Unable to sell them for cash, Alex had taken merchandise in trade, and to dispose of the goods he had been forced to open an Oriental merchandise store in San Francisco.

It was on this base that Starbuck had built his business empire, which by the time of his death had grown to span the globe. The success of the little store led to his first major expansion from Oriental goods to general merchandise, and from that point the growth that multiplied the Starbuck enterprises had begun. Other retail stores had followed the first one, and led him into dealing as a wholesaler. Then, securing transportation for his goods had gotten him involved in railroads and ocean shipping.

When he saw that he'd need financing for his railroads and shipping lines, Alex had bought a seat on the New York Stock Exchange and later added banking to his other enterprises. To secure the raw materials needed to build tracks and coaches, locomotives and steel-hulled steamships; he'd moved into mining and foundries.

Soon the Starbuck enterprises spilled into Europe, and his expansion there resulted in a series of collisions with a tight, unscrupulous international cartel, which Alex outmaneuvered in deal after deal. As the cartel's losses from the competition of the aggressive American increased, its masters set out to eliminate Alex, and ultimately succeeded in bringing about his assassination.

After the death of Jessica's mother, Alex Starbuck had never considered remarriage. He'd brought up Jessie himself, training her as he would have trained a son to take over the Starbuck enterprises after his death. Neither of them had anticipated that death would take Alex so early, nor that it would be at the hands of a team of killers hired by the international cabal.

Sitting in her father's deep leather-upholstered chair, the fragrance of his cherry-flavored pipe tobacco still clinging to the well-worn cushions, Jessie closed her eyes and leaned back for a moment as memories, glad and sad, flowed through her mind. Then she straightened up and rolled the top of the desk open. Reaching into the pigeonhole that only she and Ki knew held the latch of the secret drawer built into the desk, Jessie opened the concealed drawer. Lying on top of a small stack of confidential reports and notes was

Alex's small black notebook containing the data his agents had uncovered regarding the histories and habits of the cartel's top members.

Jessie thumbed through the dog-eared pages until she found the entry she was seeking. Her memory had been correct. There, in a condensed version of her father's flowing script, she read:

> Farnam, Joseph John, Sr.
> Boston, Mass., U.S.A.
> Res: Commonwealth Ave.; summer home Marblehead
> Wife Deborah decsd. ; Farnam never remarried but
>   mntns mistresses Birdie Ostrow, N.Y. actress;
>   Mabel Cross, former secy, Boston
> Chldn: Joseph John, Jr., Leicstr Acad., USMilAcad.;
>   Constance, m. Rbt. Higham; Lynn, m. Ward
>   Peabody
> Bus. offcs Mayflower Ntl Bnk Bldg, State St.; clubs,
>   Somerset, City, Union
> Pol: R
> Textiles, felting, shoes, coal, RR; financed short sales
>   B&VRR stock, took control B&V after bnkrptcy
>   w/ Henri Duclos, Belg., Augustus Schertz,
>   Ger.; Farnam new member cartel; Farnam,
>   Duclos, Schertz constrct rt-of-way Starbuck RRs
>   Ohio, Penna., Montana Terr.; suspct sabotage
>   train Toledo.

Jessie read the entry twice, trying to read into it more than Alex's often-cryptic abbreviations revealed. She went to the entries covering Duclos of Belgium and Schertz of Germany. These two had crossed swords with Alex more than once over the years, but Farnam's name was not mentioned in connection with other clashes between her father and the cartel.

It can't be coincidence, though, Jessie mused. *There simply couldn't be another lieutenant named Joe Farnam who graduated from West Point. And a young officer who's the son of a man like Farnam usually gets a more comfortable assignment than Fort Chaplin. So, if it can't be coincidence, there's got to be a reason. And the only reason that makes sense is some scheme the cartel's trying to carry out.*

After rereading the Farnam entry, Jessica restored Alex's notebook to its hiding place and closed the secret drawer. She leaned back in the big leather chair and closed her eyes, trying to think of any possible connection that could be made between the cartel and the rustling of Brad Close's market herd. She was on the point of falling asleep when the scattered factors came together and brought her awake with a start.

Jessica stood up and glanced at the Vienna pendulum clock that hung on the wall over Alex's desk. Even though it was past midnight, she ran up the stairs and tapped on Ki's door. When he opened it, she whispered, "We've got to talk tonight about the Box B herd being rustled, Ki."

"Tonight? Can't it wait until tomorrow?"

"No. We need to go over my idea right now."

Ki nodded. "You wouldn't be in such a hurry if it weren't important. I'll be right down."

"In Alex's study. I'll start some water boiling. We'll both want tea."

By the time Ki came into the study, water was boiling in the miniature two-cup kettle over the flame of the spirit-burner that was always kept ready on its stand in a corner of the room. Jessie had just opened a tin of tea, and its subtle aroma was stealing through the air.

Ki sniffed appreciatively. "Ah, Cloud Mist. Perfect for a late-night conference."

"That's what I thought, too."

Jessie put a pinch of the tea into the cups she'd gotten out and poured the boiling water into them. The fragrance of the steeping tea rose from the cups. She handed one to Ki and took the other to the desk, where she sat down in the big leather chair. Ki took his cup to the sofa and sat down facing her.

"What is this idea you have, Jessie?"

"It may be farfetched, Ki, but it's the only thing I can think of that makes sense. If I'm right, rustling the Box B herd is just the start of something much, much bigger."

"There's more to it than just a gang of bandits from Mexico starting the old Laredo Loop again, then?"

"Perhaps. That's what we'll have to find out. But I've gotten very suspicious of coincidences."

Quickly, Jessie outlined for Ki what she'd found concerning the Farnam family in her father's notebook. When she'd finished, Ki shook his head.

"I still don't see what you're driving at, Jessie."

"I don't think it's a coincidence that a young lieutenant named Joe Farnam was suddenly placed in command at Fort Chaplin, Ki. Especially at the same time the army changed its policy of helping ranchers along the border to deal with rustlers who come across the Rio Grande from Mexico."

Ki said thoughtfully, "Policy is made in Washington, of course. That would mean that Farnam's father could have had a hand in it, I suppose."

"He had enough influence to get his son accepted at West Point. And it's no secret that the army's very vulnerable to political influence right now. Besides, the senior Joseph Farnam can use not only his own political strength, he can call on the other cartel members in this country as well."

"But for what purpose, Jessie?"

"Something you said earlier today gave me the idea, Ki."

Ki thought for a moment, then shook his head, frowning. "It must have been some remark I've forgotten, then."

"When we were first talking about the rustlers, you said the Lazy G or the Circle Star might be next on their list."

"Even if they stole one of our market herds, they couldn't hurt the Circle Star, Jessie. Not the way losing a herd hurts Brad Close's Box B."

"Of course not." Jessie raised her teacup to her lips, and found it empty. She picked up Ki's cup, which was empty too, and went to the stand. As she refilled the miniature teapot and relighted the spirit lamp, she went on talking.

"We could survive, as you said this afternoon, Ki. And you were right about the Lazy G, too. The syndicate got three million acres of land in ten counties for building the Texas capital, and the Lazy G's just a little part of those three million acres."

"Then what's your point?"

"This is our headquarters, Ki."

"Jessie," Ki said patiently, "even if we lost the Circle Star as a headquarters, we have others we can use."

Before he'd finished speaking, the look in Jessie's emerald-green eyes told Ki he'd said the wrong thing. In spite of the angry gleam her eyes showed, Jessie held her temper.

She said, "I know as well as you do that we can work out of the other bases we have. But they aren't the same as the Circle Star, Ki. This is more than a base or a headquarters to work from. This is home!"

"I'm sorry, Jessie. I know you feel just the way Alex did about the ranch. And you're right, of course. But what I said about our not having to worry over the loss of one market herd still makes sense, doesn't it?"

Jessie came back with the cups of freshly brewed tea. She said, "In one way it does, but if you carry that thought a step further, it can be really alarming."

"Carry it further in what direction?"

"In a ring around the Circle Star. Our neighbors, the ones that touch our range."

"That means the Box B, the Lazy G, the Lightning Fork, and the X Slash X," Ki frowned. "But I still don't see what you're trying to tell me."

"Think, Ki!" Jessie urged. "What would our situation be if we couldn't drive a market herd from the Circle Star across the range that belongs to any of those four ranches?"

"Why, we wouldn't be able to get our cattle off Circle Star land, of course," Ki replied promptly.

"Suppose the rustlers who stole the Box B herd never took a single steer off the Circle Star range, but came back and stripped the Lazy G and the Lightning Fork and the X Slash X, not all at once, but one at a time?"

40

Ki frowned thoughtfully. "Well, we've both agreed the Lazy G wouldn't be hurt much. From what I last heard, the Lightning Fork's in good condition. The X Slash X is in about the same shape as the Box B, though. Shaky."

"Now suppose the rustlers came back every few months, not just when the market herds are formed."

"Jessie, you know that if that happened, every hand on all these ranches would join forces and wipe out the rustlers. And we'd be right with them, leading the Circle Star men."

"How long do you think a cattle ranch can survive if it has to fight a constant war with rustlers, Ki? How long would Brad Close or the X Slash X last under those conditions?"

"Brad might hold on another year. The X Slash X—well, two years, maybe three."

"And how long do you think it would take the capital syndicate to decide they'd better get rid of the Lazy G?"

"They're Eastern promoters, not Texas cattlemen. They'd sell out to anybody who made them an offer."

"Where would the Circle Star be then?"

"Surrounded by strangers."

"Or the cartel."

Ki stared at her, his mouth open. Then he said slowly, "Do you really think—"

"Yes I do. As long as there's a Starbuck here, the Circle Star will be one of their prime targets."

"I suppose the cartel could have gotten the idea of starting the old Laredo Loop up again," Ki frowned. "It wouldn't be too hard for them to get a bunch of rustlers together in Mexico, outlaws who'd know how the Loop works."

"Remember what Brad said this evening. There are plenty of men in Mexico with guns for hire."

"But doing what you've dreamed up would take them years!"

"You know how the cartel works, Ki. They don't count time and costs, as long as they see a chance to win in the end."

Ki nodded thoughtfully. "Yes. They've already proved

41

that by the years and the money they spent fighting your father."

"And if I can imagine a plan like the one I've just told you about, they can too. They're not stupid."

"No. They're not. It wouldn't take them long, either, if they really are working on the kind of scheme you described."

"Even if it cost them a fortune, they'd wind up owning a spread bigger than the capital syndicate got," Jessie pointed out. "They'd make money, in the long run."

"And they'd have—" Ki stopped short.

"They'd have eliminated the Starbucks," Jessie finished for him, her voice bitter.

"Yes. But I can't see you just letting them get away with it."

"Oh, we're going to fight. Even if everything I've talked about is just a wild dream, something I've imagined could happen, we'll fight."

"That's hardly a surprise, Jessie. The question is how."

"We'll have to find out who and what we're fighting, first."

"A trip to Mexico?"

"Yes. But first, a visit to Fort Chaplin."

"To investigate Lieutenant Joseph Farnam?"

"I'm sure that when we do, we'll find out there's a 'Junior' after his name."

"Brad might be able to tell us that," Ki suggested.

"Perhaps. But I don't want Brad to know anything about our plans. Or what we've been talking about tonight."

Ki nodded. "There'd be no way of stopping him, if he found out what we're planning."

"He's not in any condition to go back to Mexico, Ki. A trip like that would more than likely kill him."

"When do we leave?"

"It'll take us most of tomorrow to get ready. We can't even begin to make any plans until Brad starts back to the Box B."

42

"Fort Chaplin's a long day's ride from here, Jessie," Ki reminded her.

Jessie shrugged. "We've made long day's rides before. And will again, I'm sure."

"Day after tomorrow, then?"

"Yes," Jessie agreed. "Day after tomorrow, at daybreak."

★

Chapter 5

"Unless I'm wrong, we'll be in sight of Fort Chaplin before sundown," Ki told Jessie across the coals of the small fire he'd kindled for their noonday meal.

They both sat with folded legs, facing one another across what was left of the small, wood-conserving fire over which Ki was boiling water for their noon tea. Jessie wore her range clothing: tight, well-broken-in denim jeans and jacket, a tan silk blouse, boots of glove-soft leather, and for the brief stop she had not discarded her brown Stetson, but had pushed it back off her head to dangle at her back. Ki wore his own version of travel togs, which were similar to Jessie's except that his shirt was a loose, collarless cotton twill pullover, and he wore the canvas slippers he favored in place of boots.

A pan of water sitting on the coals was just coming to a boil. Ki swirled a few drops of the steaming water in the small teapot he carried in his saddlebags, poured the water out, added a large pinch of tea leaves, and filled the teapot. Then he set the pot beside the coals to let the tea steep.

Jessie ate the last bite of the vinegared rice balls with bits of chicken that they'd packed along for their nooning. "I'll be glad to get there, even though I don't suppose the scenery will be any more attractive than it is here," she said. "But it will be the first step to getting our questions answered."

Ki hunkered down beside her. He said, "I'm not sure about that. We might be better off ignoring this Lieutenant Farnam and going right on to Mexico."

45

"We've already talked about that, Ki. I thought it was all settled."

"It was. Is, I suppose."

Jessie took the cup that Ki handed her, and while he filled it from the steaming teapot, she said, "I don't see why you're so impatient, Ki. Unless we stay a step ahead of the cartel, they could take us by surprise when they start carrying out whatever plan they have in mind."

Ki rarely allowed his Oriental fatalism to surface, but this time he replied by quoting a line from an ode by Li'tai Po: "The fighting and the attacking are without a time of ending."

Jessie sat silently for a moment before she answered, "There will be an ending someday, Ki. But it must be at the time when we've beaten them, and on our terms."

"Only a fool would contradict that, Jessie," Ki replied. "And you've led us back to where we started. If the suspicions you told me you have are correct, we'd better be moving instead of sitting here talking."

"You're right, of course," Jessie agreed.

She stood up and stretched to relax the muscles that kept reminding her of the hours she'd spent in the saddle. Ki picked up the utensils and cups and returned them to his saddlebag. He made a stirrup of his hands to help Jessie mount. Jessie put her booted foot in the stirrup and settled into her saddle. They headed southwest on the almost-obliterated army wagon road that led to Fort Chaplin.

An almost imperceptible tinge of pink in the west gave warning of the day's impending end when they came in sight of the fort's decrepit buildings. Constructed during the short war in 1846 between the United States and Mexico over possession of New Mexico and Arizona territories, Fort Chaplin was one of the few military installations that still remained active along the Rio Grande.

Reining in, they inspected the fort. Obviously, little had been done to maintain it. The adobe bricks that once surrounded the buildings had eroded during the years to a dike of ocher earth that now stood less than two feet high in the least damaged spots. It now served only as a defining line.

Inside the square it enclosed, nothing remained but part of a barracks, a portion of a building that had once been officers' quarters, the low stone curb of a well, and most of the original stables. A few soldiers in faded blues moved between the stable and the barracks; they abandoned whatever they were doing and stared openly at Jessie and Ki as they reined in.

There was a small hut at one side of the former parade ground; a flag drooped from its staff in front of the small building. As they watched, a soldier came to the door and looked out, then disappeared inside again.

"That must be the headquarters," she said.

Ki nodded. "Yes. And now, once more, we become mistress and servant. I'll keep in the background, as always, but you'll know I'm watching and ready if you run into trouble."

They stepped their horses over the hump of the former wall and rode up to the hut. Ki dismounted first and, aware of the eyes of the soldiers still fixed on them, held Jessie's horse while she swung out of her saddle and went into the little building.

Inside, the still-harsh sunlight of the late afternoon was tempered to a bearable glow though the high, small windows that were in the room's two side walls. A soldier wearing the stripes of a lance corporal was seated at a table, writing. He looked up when Jessie came in, and managed to hide most of his surprise when he saw that the visitor was a young and pretty woman.

"Ma'am," he said, putting down his pen and standing up. "May I help you?"

"I'm looking for Lieutenant Farnam," Jessie replied. She pushed her hat back and shook out her gleaming reddish blond hair, aware of the admiring glances that the young lance corporal was trying to keep from being too obvious.

"Why, he's out at the stables right now, but I'll be glad to go get him, if you don't mind waiting."

Jessie treated the soldier to one of her dazzling smiles.

"If you would, please. You might tell him that Jessica Starbuck would like to talk with him."

"I sure will, ma'am. If you'd like to sit down..."

"I'll find a chair if I do. But after a long ride, I think I prefer to walk around a bit and stretch my legs."

"Yes, ma'am," the soldier replied without taking his eyes off her. He backed away from the table and sidled out of the small room.

Jessie took stock of her surroundings. A row of wooden filing cabinets lined one wall of the small building, but from the dust that lay on the documents piled on their tops, the edges of the drawers and the handles, Jessie could see they had not been touched for months.

She turned her attention to the boxes that stood against the other wall. They too were overflowing with sheets of paper, and she stepped over to look at them. As she'd deduced, they were current: copies of informal patrol reports, and of the more formal versions of the same reports that had been sent to corps headquarters; payroll records; muster sheets; copies of the fort's cash accounts.

She heard the grating of footsteps on the baked ground outside and stepped away from the boxes. She was standing idly beside the table when the lieutenant entered, followed by the lance corporal.

Farnam wore the gray shirt and red-striped blue trousers of the cavalry's barracks uniform. He was bareheaded, and his crisp black hair curled down his cheeks in wide sideburns, ending just above the line of his square, firm chin. He did not have a mustache. His eyes were a clear brown, his lips full. Jessie guessed his age as the late twenties or perhaps the early thirties. His skin was just beginning to acquire the deep tan that went with outdoor service.

"Miss Starbuck," the lieutenant said. He put his heels together and inclined his torso forward almost exactly forty-five degrees; Jessie recognized the bow as a trademark of the West Point graduate. "Lieutenant Joseph Farnam, Junior, ma'am, at your service."

48

"Lieutenant Farnam," Jessie said, extending her hand. She was watching the lieutenant closely for a reaction to her presence, but he seemed to accept as a less than unusual event the unexpected arrival of a woman visitor.

Farnam bowed over the hand, his lips not quite touching it, another West Point trademark. When he straightened up, he said, "This is quite a surprise, Miss Starbuck. I've heard of your famous ranch, of course, but haven't yet had the time to make courtesy calls on any of the ranches hereabouts."

Jessie replied, "You'll be welcome anytime you stop to visit us, of course, Lieutenant. I'm sure you know where the Circle Star is located."

"In the short time I've been stationed here, I've heard a great deal about the famous Starbuck ranch. And I hope your visit isn't to report that you're having trouble there."

"There's no trouble at the Circle Star that would require the army's attention, Lieutenant Farnam." Jessie paused before embarking on her plans. She said, "Before I go into the reason for my visit, Lieutenant, let me ask you if it's possible for you to provide my servant and me with a bite of dinner and a place to sleep tonight."

"Why, certainly. I'd have asked you to be our guest in any event, Miss Starbuck. This wild country isn't the safest place for two travelers, one a young lady, even in daylight."

"This wild country is home to me, Lieutenant. But like anyone else, I'd prefer to sleep in a bed when one's available, rather than on the ground."

"We don't have special guest quarters," Farnam told her. "But with a reduced roster, there are spare rooms in both the officers' quarters and what's left of the barracks. Your man can sleep there and eat at the enlisted men's mess. And I'll be honored to have you join me for dinner, such as it might be."

"I don't want to put you to any extra trouble..."

"Nonsense!" Farnam turned to the lance corporal. "Tompkins, you will see to preparing quarters for Miss

49

Starbuck, and tell her man he can sleep in the barracks. Have the hostler take care of their horses, and put Miss Starbuck's saddlebags in the room you prepare for her."

"Really, Lieutenant Farnam, you don't have to go to all this trouble," Jessie protested.

"No trouble at all," Farnam said over his shoulder before continuing his instructions to Tompkins. "Tell the mess sergeant I'm having a lady guest for dinner, and see if he can provide something besides salt beef and boiled potatoes." With a salute, the soldier departed on his errand. Farnam returned his attention to Jessica. "I'm still curious about the purpose of your visit, Miss Starbuck, but I have a duty to command the evening muster in less than a quarter of an hour. If nothing too urgent has brought you here, I suggest that we postpone discussing the reason for your visit until later. Over dinner?"

"That would be very nice, Lieutenant. And please don't feel that you have to give me any kind of special attention."

"Our musters here are very brief," Farnam said. "I only hold them because regulations require me to. But if you'd like to watch . . ."

"I wouldn't want to interfere with your duties, Lieutenant Farnam. And I'd like a few minutes to freshen up before dinner."

"Of course. I'm going to my quarters now, to get my sword. Another regulation, and here at Fort Chaplin, a useless one, I think. But Tompkins should have a room ready for you by now, so if you'll allow me to escort you . . ."

Jessie walked beside Farnam to the officers' quarters, where an open door with a small heap of used bedding piled outside it helped Farnam to identify the room that was being readied for her. Tompkins came out just as she and Farnam arrived. He saluted.

"Everything's taken care of, sir," he reported to Farnam. "And I told Coffee to serve supper for two in your quarters, sir. He says not to worry."

"Good," Farnam said. He bowed to Jessie again. "Until

later, then, Miss Starbuck. I'll call for you when dinner's ready."

Jessie found the room as characterless as she'd expected it to be, but much cleaner. A narrow iron bedstead stood in the center of the wall opposite the door. The small chamber's remaining pieces of furniture—a table, two chairs, and a mirrorless four-drawer bureau—were set in the exact centers of the walls on each side of that occupied by the bed. Jessie's saddlebags had been placed beside the bureau, on which a white china washbowl stood, a large pitcher beside it.

Glancing into the pitcher, Jessie found that it had been filled with water. She sat down in one of the chairs and looked at the bed; a china chamberpot shoved discreetly under it caught her eye. She noted that the bed had been spread with fresh sheets, clean but unironed, and had been made with military precision. The coarse gray army blanket was folded with geometric care at right angles to the sides, the pillow set exactly in the center at the head.

Jessie's thoughts returned to her brief encounter with Lieutenant Farnam in the headquarters building. His lack of surprise when she and Ki had made their unexpected appearance could mean one of two things, she decided. Either he was unaware of his father's connection with the cartel and its efforts to wipe out the Starbuck enterprises, or he was capable of playing a very deep game of deception.

Farnam did not have the look of a man skilled in dissimulation, her thoughts ran on, nor did he behave like one. But dinner and a few carefully phrased but seemingly casual questions should give her the answers she was seeking.

A small smile playing on her lips, Jessie took a bar of soap, a clean washcloth, and a small silver flask of cologne from her saddlebags. Standing up, she poured water into the washbowl. When Lieutenant Farnam rapped lightly at her door ten minutes later, she was ready to step out and greet him with a smile.

"It's very kind of you to accommodate a total stranger

51

who appeared without any notice," she told him as they walked the few steps along the veranda to his quarters.

"You're the one who's being kind, Miss Starbuck. I've been getting bored with my own company for the past several days."

Before Jessie could comment, Farnam opened the door to his quarters and stood aside for her to enter. The room was half office, half living room; a second door, in the center of the wall at right angles to the entrance, stood ajar, indicating to Jessie that the fort's commander had more than a single room. A table stood in the room's center, bearing place-settings and a steaming tureen. Farnam seated Jessie and took his place across from her.

"I suspect that some of the troopers have been violating standing orders by using military ammunition for hunting," he said with a smile. "At any rate, we're having rabbit stew."

For the first few minutes after Farnam had served their plates, they ate in silence; Jessie found the stew surprisingly good. After the edge had been taken off their appetites, she asked, "Are you the only commissioned officer at the fort, Lieutenant Farnam? I thought there were enough men here to require several officers."

"There are," he replied. "But both of my second lieutenants are out with patrols, and have been for the past week. It's possible that they won't return for another week, perhaps longer. Since regulations don't permit me to eat with the enlisted men unless we're in the field, I've had to dine alone."

Given the opening Farnam had just provided, Jessie chose to ask at once the question that had popped into her mind, instead of making polite chitchat.

She said, "Two patrols out at once? Isn't that somewhat unusual, when you have so few men on duty here?"

"Regulations again, Miss Starbuck. I'm required to see that each enlisted man and officer spends a prescribed number of days on patrol duty."

"I see. It occurred to me that the patrols might have some connection with the rustlers from Mexico that stole a large herd of cattle from one of my neighbors about two weeks ago."

"You're referring to Mr. Bradford Close's Box B ranch?"

"Yes. Brad's a good neighbor of mine. When he told me—"

Farnam's lips had been slowly compressing as Jessie spoke. Now he interrupted angrily. "Miss Starbuck, I understand that you ranchers stick together. But the army doesn't like spies who sneak into its forts under false pretenses, even when there's no war going on! And from what I gather, you're here to spy!"

Jessie stared in undisguised astonishment at the lieutenant. Before she could decide what to say in reply to his outburst, Farnam recovered his poise.

"I'm sorry, Miss Starbuck," he said contritely. "That was uncalled for on my part. Please accept my apologies."

"I'm not sure that I want to, Lieutenant Farnam," Jessie told him levelly, keeping both surprise and anger from her voice. "All I can think of is that you must be something more than bored by the enforced seclusion you mentioned a few minutes ago."

"I'll admit my nerves are a bit on edge," Farnam said. "More so than I realized, I suppose. I do apologize, quite humbly and very sincerely."

Jessie pressed her advantage. "Don't you think I'm entitled to an explanation for what you just said?"

"Yes, you are," Farnam replied promptly. "But I'm not sure that I can give you one."

"I'm afraid I don't understand, Lieutenant."

"I—" Farnam began, then stopped short. He gestured at the dinner table. "Do you care for anything more, Miss Starbuck? I think I've lost my appetite."

"I've had quite enough, thank you," Jessie answered. She took her napkin from her lap, folded it and placed it on the table, and made a move to stand up.

"No, no," Farnam protested. "I don't want you to end the evening until I've made amends for my unfortunate remarks. I think a glass of brandy might help settle my nerves, and I was hoping you'd like one, too."

Not really wanting to leave, anxious to ask Farnam still more questions while his mind was preoccupied with something else, Jessie told him, "I'd enjoy a bit of brandy, and if it will settle your nerves to the point where you can give me an explanation for your accusation, I'll stay and have one with you."

"Thank you." Farnam went to a small cellarette that stood in a corner of the room. He said, "I'm afraid that all I can offer you is Otard. The finer French liquors don't get to this part of the world."

"Otard will be very satisfactory," Jessie replied. She made a move to get up, and Lieutenant Farnam hurried to pull her chair back from the table.

"We can have our brandy on the veranda," he suggested. "I might find it a bit easier to talk outside. This room"—he waved at its bareness—"may have something to do with my state of mind."

"If you'd prefer that," she answered, her voice cool and unsympathetic.

Farnam moved chairs out to the narrow veranda. The moon was high now, and full, its glow softening the harshness of the terrain visible from the veranda. Farnam poured brandy into glasses and offered one of them to Jessie. When he turned his back to her to pick up his drink, Jessie saw him empty the glass in a single gulp and refill it quickly. She looked out across the fort's grounds at the glowing windows of the barracks, and was still watching them when Farnam turned around.

"It is better out here, isn't it?" he asked.

Jessie turned back to face him as he struck a match to light his cigar. In the flickering of the match, Jessie saw that his face bore a worried frown.

"Yes. It's quite pleasant in the moonlight."

"Too bad things don't look the same in daylight," Farnam

said. His voice was harsh. He drained his glass as quickly as he'd gulped the first, then stepped back to the table and filled it again. Then he came back to the chair and sat down facing Jessie. She said nothing, but took a sip of brandy, her eyes still focused on the fort's moonlit grounds.

They sat silently for a few moments before Farnam said, "I'm not quite sure what caused me to blurt out the totally uncalled-for remark for which I've already apologized, Miss Starbuck, but during the past two weeks I've been under something of a strain."

"I think I understand the feeling, Lieutenant," Jessie said. Then, to bring the discussion to a point quickly, she went on, "Luckily, my father prepared me to face the fact that being in command of anything, whether it's a business enterprise or a ranch, or anything involving a number of individuals, requires an ability to set aside facts that might be personally unpleasant and come to grips with hard realities."

"Your father and mine must be quite different sorts of men, then," Farnam remarked. Though he tried to make his comment sound casual, Jessie detected a bitterness in his voice.

"My father's dead, Lieutenant," Jessie said quietly. "I've been managing the Starbuck enterprises myself for some time."

"I see," Farnam said. In the glow of his cigar tip, Jessie watched his face knitting into a frown. He no longer tried to conceal the bitterness in his words as he went on, "It sounds harsh when I put it into words, but I sometimes wish my father were dead, too. Then I'd be relieved of the constant pressure I'm under to give up my army career and join him in his business operations, for which I have no liking at all."

Jessie suppressed her urge to start asking questions at once. Instead, she sipped her brandy and, in a manner that suggested sympathy rather than curiosity, said, "Sometimes it helps to talk about problems with strangers, Lieutenant."

"I don't want to spoil your evening by boring you with

my personal problems, Miss Starbuck." Farnam paused, then added, "But if you wouldn't mind . . . you understand, this is something I can't even mention to anyone on the post."

"Of course I understand," Jessie assured him in a carefully neutral tone. "And if it'll help you, I'll be glad to listen."

★

Chapter 6

Lieutenant Farnam took his time in beginning. He went to the small table where the brandy bottle stood, and after Jessie had shaken her head in response to his wordless offer to refill her glass, he poured into his own before returning to sit down.

"I'm sure you've already gathered from my remarks that only part of the strain I was referring to a moment ago is connected with my position as commander here at Fort Chaplin." He paused for several seconds before going on, "You know, Miss Starbuck, at the Point we were taught the meaning of what our instructors called 'command decisions,' which involve leading men, sending them into danger. Unfortunately I didn't get this kind of education from my father on making my own personal decisions."

"And your family ties are getting strained, with you so far from home?"

"I suppose that's as good a way as any to put it," Farnam said. "You're quick to grasp a point, Miss Starbuck. But you're quite right. You see, Father didn't approve at all of my ambition to make a career in the army. He wanted me to follow him in taking charge of the family's business affairs."

Jessie was not one to let pass such an inviting opportunity to confirm her initial suspicion regarding the senior Farnam's connection with the cartel. She asked, "Just what is your father's business, Lieutenant?"

"Oh, Father's involved in several fields," Farnam answered. "Felt and textile mills, a factory or two, mining, railroads. But a life in the business world never appealed to me. As long as I can remember, all I've been interested in is the army."

Jessie felt frustrated; Farnam's disclaimer did not coincide with the mental picture she'd been painting. However, she was sure that, thanks to Alex Starbuck's careful tutoring, she was able to distinguish between truth and lies. She said, "So you disregarded your father's wishes and made the army your career?"

"Yes. Not without some open unpleasantness, of course. But Father never did approve. One of the reasons I asked to be stationed here on the Rio Grande was to get as far away from home as possible."

"Where is home, Lieutenant Farnam?"

"Boston."

Though she'd been sure for several minutes that her guesses about Farnam's parentage had been correct, Jessie considered his reply a final confirmation. She dismissed the subject by saying lightly, "You're about as far from there as you can get and still stay in the United States."

"That was my idea. But the mail can still reach me here."

"You've been getting letters recently, I take it?"

"Constantly. Two or three in every mail delivery—which is once every two weeks, thanks to the size of the state of Texas."

"It should be easy enough for you to hold your own, Lieutenant Farnam."

"You don't know my father, Miss Starbuck. He can be very emphatic. Lately he's lost patience. Now he's beginning to hint that if I don't do what he wants me to, he'll use his connections in Washington to hinder my army career."

"Would he do that to his own son?"

"Yes. I'm sure he would. I know my father that well."

"Well." Jessie sat silently after the one thoughtful word, then she said, "I can understand your nervous strain now, Lieutenant Farnam. I accept your apology. Suppose we forget that the little incident ever happened and start over, as friends. And to begin with, you might try calling me Jessie."

"You're really serious, aren't you?" Farnam asked, his voice much lighter. "Thank you, Miss... Jessie. My name's Joseph, but my friends call me Joe, as you might expect."

"We're in agreement, then, Joe." Jessie raised her glass, which was still half full. "To friendship."

"To friendship," Farnam repeated. After they'd sipped their brandy, he said, "I'm not completely naive, Jessie. You must have had a reason for stopping here, and I have an idea you came to talk about the rustlers that stripped the Box B ranch."

Jessie decided it was time to come to the point. "Yes. Brad Close stopped by my ranch several days ago. He was returning from the fort, and he told me about the new army regulations that bar you from helping ranchers—or any other civilians, I suppose—unless there's a war or an invasion."

"I didn't make the regulations, Jessie, and I'm not in sympathy with them myself. I don't have any choice but to obey them, though."

"Oh, I understand that. But as far as the ranchers along the border are concerned, there's really no difference between rustlers and the Mexican army crossing the Rio Grande. We think one is as much of an invasion as the other."

"Unfortunately, Washington doesn't take that attitude."

"Washington's attitudes can be changed, Joe," Jessie told him somewhat brusquely. "The Starbuck name has a good deal of influence there."

Farnam did not reply at once. Finally he said, "How would you go about changing those regulations, Jessie?"

"Joe," Jessie said quietly, "Starbuck enterprises cover a great deal of territory. We contribute quite generously to the campaign funds of senators and congressmen from more than twenty of the thirty-eight states. Need I say more than that?"

Farnam shook his head. "No. I didn't realize that your family interests were so widespread. I'm sure you can do what you say. But you must have had something in mind that's brought you here, Jessie. This isn't just a casual visit. What is it that you want me to do to help you?"

Jessie and Ki had discussed several specific items on their trip from the Circle Star. Now Jessie said, "I'm sure there aren't too many places along this stretch of the Rio Grande where cattle can be herded across easily. You must know where they are. I hope you'll give me the details I need to use when we begin putting pressure on the army through Congress."

After a moment's thought, Farnam told Jessie, "I only know of two places in the Fort Chaplin area where it would be easy to get a cattle herd across the river. At least those are the only two spots my scouts have pointed out to me. If I show them to you on a map—"

"No," Jessie interrupted. "I need to know more about those places than I can learn from looking at a map, Joe. Do you have enough men to spare so that you could assign one of them to ride with Ki and me, so that we can actually see these places you're talking about?"

"I'll do better than that," Farnam said promptly. "I need to get out of this place for a few days, and Lieutenant Mitchell, my second-in-command, is due back from patrol tomorrow. How would it be if I guided you myself?"

Jessie's acceptance was as prompt as Farnam's offer. "I'd like it very much, Joe." She frowned and went on, "You said a few days. How far is it?"

"Both of the fords lie south of the fort. The nearest is a bit more than a half-day's ride. The other's a good twenty miles beyond the first. Your Texas distances are incredible, Jessie."

"They are until you get used to them," she smiled. "But this is important enough to me to spend that much time on. You said your second lieutenants are due back soon. Must you wait until they get here, or can we start early in the morning?"

"I don't see why I should wait for Mitchell to show up," Farnam said. "My first sergeant, Henderson, is perfectly capable of keeping the routine going for the short time that the fort would be without a commissioned officer in command. It'd only be for a few hours at most, until Mitchell gets back." Farnam hesitated and added, "There's one thing I should tell you, though. Regulations again, as you might suppose. Standing orders say that military personnel must not go into Mexico, even if we're in pursuit of hostiles."

"I wouldn't expect you to disobey army orders, Joe. If you'll just take Ki and me to the fords, we'll do any investigating that's necessary on the Mexican side of the river."

"This is something I simply can't believe," Farnam said, his puzzlement plain in his tone. "For some reason, this ford isn't marked on my map. It isn't on the master map at the fort, either, or I'd remember it."

"Your mapmaker is careless," Ki suggested. "This ford has been used many times, Lieutenant, and not long ago. There are fresh cattle tracks and the tracks of the riders driving them on the opposite bank as well as on this one."

"I don't question that, Ki," Farnam said. "Little as I know about tracking, I can tell the difference between the tracks of steers and those of shod horses."

Farnam, Ki, and Jessie were sitting their horses beside the Rio Grande; the legs of Ki's horse were still dripping from his exploration of the unmapped crossing they'd discovered. All three of them sat in silence for a moment as they gazed at the surface of the river, darkening now as the steep cliffs on the opposite bank began to shade the water from the afternoon sun.

When the long day had started at Fort Chaplin, the trio had ridden in the silence common to either good companions or to strangers traveling together for the first time. As the morning wore on, they'd lost the stiffness that had marked the beginning of their journey. During their noon stop to eat the sandwiches prepared by the fort's mess sergeant,

61

Jessie and Farnam had chatted almost as friends, while Ki maintained his role as Jessie's servant and kept discreetly silent.

As the afternoon progressed, Jessie had become aware that the lieutenant was glancing at her more and more often, but she'd managed to avert her eyes in time to keep him from noticing that she'd been covertly looking at him, as well.

There'll be time later, she'd told herself. *Though if I do decide, I'll have to find a way to signal Ki without Joe noticing. And Ki will understand, of course. Ki always understands.*

It had been Ki's sharp eyes that had noticed the faint tracks in the baked earth, leading them to the crossing at which they were now looking. At first, Farnam had insisted that the tracks led to the first ford across the Rio Grande, the crossing some twenty miles from the fort, which they'd already passed after finding no evidence that it had been used by cattle lately.

But Ki had persisted in urging that the tracks be followed, in spite of the military map Farnam carried, which showed impassable, broken country stretching two miles or more from the riverbank, and showed also that through that stretch of rough terrain the Rio Grande flowed through a gorge where high banks made fording the stream out of the question. Jessie, knowing Ki's skill at reading trail signs, joined Ki in wanting to discover where the cattle tracks led.

Farnam at last agreed, and the trail Ki followed had brought them to the mouth of one of a score or more of narrow arroyos, all looking alike. For almost two miles the narrow slit in the sunbaked earth through which they rode led them on a tortuous, zigzag course. There were cattle droppings in the sandy soil on the floor of the steep-walled arroyo, but even Ki's practiced eyes could not reveal the age of the cow dung.

Then, suddenly, the metal-hard caliche soil on which the hooves of their horses had grated gave way to earth that was still the light yellow of the baked caliche, but softer underfoot. Here the cattle tracks showed plainly, and after another half-mile the steep sides of the arroyo widened into a respectably broad valley that stretched at its widest perhaps a quarter-mile from one steep wall to the equally steep wall on its opposite side. They reined in at the point where the arroyo widened.

Ki pointed. "There," he said. "And there. Campfires have burned in both places, Lieutenant."

"Can you tell how long ago?" Farnam had asked.

"Not from here," Ki replied. "But I will be able to when we get closer, when I can feel the coals and the earth beneath."

"They'll be fresh, I'll bet," Jessie had put in. "Some of these tracks are only a few weeks old."

"How can you tell?" Farnam asked. "They all look alike, as far as I can see."

"Jessie is right," Ki affirmed. "Most of the prints have sharp edges, and their bottoms are not baked hard, as the old prints are. And close to the cliffs, where the sun touches the ground for only a short time each day, the dung of many of the droppings is still green; it is not yet bleached and faded. Yes, Lieutenant Farnam, cattle have been here a short while ago."

"Rustlers, you think?" Farnam asked.

"Of course!" Jessie replied emphatically.

"It could only be," Ki affirmed. "They would need to stop here and rest."

"Why?" Farnam asked. "Why rest here, with Mexico just on the other side of the river, where they'd be safe?"

Before Ki could reply, Jessie answered Farnam's question. "They'd have had to push the cattle hard to get here, Joe. The steers would be restless, and they'd stop to let them settle down before they herded them across the river."

"It may be that the ford is a hard one, too," Ki said. "Look at the tracks left on the bottom there, where the current is slow. They do not go straight, but slant upstream

63

against the flow. The ford may be narrow, on a ridge under the water." He toed his horse into the shallows, saying over his shoulder, "I will find this out very quickly."

Jessie and Farnam sat their horses while they watched Ki explore the ford. It was, as he'd suggested, on a narrow ridge that curved upstream, then downriver in midstream, and finally led in a straight line to the Mexican side of the stream.

It was while Ki was recrossing the Rio Grande that the lieutenant had taken out his map to study again, and had found that the arroyo through which they'd ridden was not shown on it. He was still examining the flawed map when Ki returned, and now Farnam rolled the map and replaced it in the cylindrical leather mapcase that hung from his saddlestrings.

"When we get back to the fort, the first thing I'll do is find out who's responsible for leaving this ford off our maps," he said angrily. "There's no excuse for such an error!"

"Perhaps it was made..." Jessie began, then hesitated and instead of saying what she'd intended to suggest, finished somewhat lamely, "...by a new man."

Farnam shook his head. "No. Ki's right. Someone was careless. And that carelessness could have cost lives."

"As it is, it's cost the Box B a valuable herd of cattle," Jessie pointed out. "If you'd known this ford was here, you might have had your patrols look at it, or even watch it."

"What good would that have done?" the lieutenant protested.

"If the rustlers knew your men came here now and then, they might be afraid to use this ford that only they seem to know about," Jessie explained.

"Rustlers who take cattle south across the river must cross to this side to steal them, too," Ki added. "They would not be able to move so freely if they had to cross at a ford that others use too."

"That hadn't occurred to me," Farnam said. "There's a

lot I still have to learn about this section of the country that I'm supposed to be responsible for protecting."

"You will, in time," Jessie assured him. "If you decide to stay in the army in spite of your father's invitaion to join him back East."

"I told you last night that I haven't any intention of doing that, Jessie," Farnam said firmly. "But that's another matter. If we're going to look at the other ford downstream, the one that does show on my map, we'd better ride out of here."

Jessie looked at the surface of the river. It shone a dull copper hue now; the high walls of the gorge through which it flowed kept the declining sun from its surface in all but a few scattered patches.

"It is getting late," she agreed. "And I'm a bit tired, after spending all day in the saddle yesterday."

"If we don't get to the downstream ford tonight, we won't be able to make the ride back to Fort Chaplin in a day," Farnam said, frowning. "But I suppose we can go part of the way before we stop, and finish the trip tomorrow. It'd mean pushing the horses rather hard, though."

"Maybe I have a better idea," Jessie said thoughtfully. "It really isn't necessary for both Ki and me to see the lay of the land around that downstream ford. If one of us gets a look at it, that's all that will be necessary." She turned to Ki and asked, "Don't you agree?"

"I only serve you," Ki said. No one except Jessie would have noticed that the bow accompanying Ki's words was half-mocking, half-serious.

"Are you too tired to ride on to the other ford now?" she asked. "You could stay there overnight, get an early start back tomorrow, and Lieutenant Farnam and I could wait for you here."

"If that is what you wish, I will be glad to do it," Ki replied.

"Would you mind very much camping here tonight, Joe?" Jessie asked Farnam.

"Why, I . . . no, of course not. We have plenty of food;

we can give Ki enough for supper and breakfast. It'll only be cold roast beef and cheese and boiled potatoes and some pickles, but that's about Fort Chaplin's limit in trail provisions."

"Oh, Ki has plenty of food in his saddlebags," Jessie said quickly. Turning to Ki, she asked, "Don't you?"

Ki nodded, and Lieutenant Farnum said, "You know, it hadn't occurred to me to split up. I wonder, though. Do you really think it's wise?"

"I don't see any reason why we shouldn't," Jessie said. "If Ki doesn't mind going to the downstream ford alone."

"I have said I will do so," Ki told her. "And perhaps it would be the best thing to do, if you feel you need to rest."

"It's settled, then," Jessie said. "You ride on downstream and scout around the other ford, Ki. You'll know what to look for. We'll look for you back here tomorrow, about midmorning, and we'll all ride back to Fort Chaplin together."

His voice mild and innocent, but his eyes holding Jessie's and showing an amused gleam, Ki asked, "You're sure you'll feel like riding back after a good night's rest?"

Equally innocently, Jessie replied, "Of course I will."

"I'd better start now, then," Ki said. "If I push my horse a little bit, I should get there before dark."

Jessie and Farnam wheeled their horses to watch Ki as he rode toward the narrow mouth leading to the arroyo. When the first bend in the winding gully hid him from view, Farnam turned to Jessie and said, "I suppose we'd better pick a place where we'll be sheltered as much as possible tonight. There are two or three splits in the canyon wall. Shall we ride along the base, and choose the one that looks best?"

"I suppose we'd better do any looking we need to before it gets dark," she answered. "And if we look closely around those two old campfires, we might find some wood the rustlers didn't burn. A fire would be nice, later on."

They walked the horses along the canyon wall, inspecting

the wide fissures that Farnam had mentioned. Only one of them was wide enough to be suitable for their purpose. It was eight or ten feet wide at the canyon floor, and tapered to a hand-wide crevice at the rim. The black and gray ashes of a fire showed that the last group passing through the canyon had used it too.

They went inside, and found that the cleft only looked shallow. It tapered down to a vee a dozen feet from its opening, but at the back it opened into a low cavern with room enough to accommodate several men. At one side of the cave, a few sticks of firewood lay in a jackstraw-like heap.

"Looks like this is just what we need," Farnam said. "We can bring the horses in and put them in the cave, though I doubt that we need to worry about them straying."

"It's perfect," Jessie agreed. "We might as well move in, as long as we're here."

"Why don't you just sit down and rest?" Farnam suggested as they walked back to the horses. "You're tired, Jessie. I'll unsaddle your horse and bring in our gear."

"I'm not too tired to take care of my own horse, Joe. And we certainly aren't going to have a lot of preparation to do, making camp."

As she spoke, Jessie was untying the saddlestrings that held her rifle scabbard. By the time she'd carried the rifle into the cleft and returned, Farnam had the saddle off her horse and was taking it to the cave. She lifted the saddlebags off his shoulder and they walked side by side through the cleft to drop their burdens.

"You don't have to baby me, Joe," she told him as they put their loads down. "Go ahead and tend to your horse now. I'll carry those sticks of firewood out, and spread our blankets."

"I . . . I thought I might ride around the canyon again and up the passageway," Farnam said hesitantly. "You . . . well, you might like a little time to yourself, before supper."

"Fine. Leave your saddlebags, and while you're riding

I'll get things in order here." She looked at the Rio Grande, its surface dark now with the sun completely off the water, and went on guilelessly, "In fact, you can take your time investigating the arroyo. The water looks so cool and inviting that I think I'll take a bath."

Chapter 7

Jessie watched Joe Farnam's broad shoulders swaying in rhythm to the pacing of his horse as he rode slowly toward the narrow end of the canyon. Never one to deceive herself, Jessie had known for the past week that it was time for another man to attract her and to be attracted to her in turn. Mere physical relief was not and had never been enough for Jessie. She needed the surge of intense feeling between herself and a man to whom she in turn felt drawn. Consequently, while she'd been fully aware of Farnam's openly admiring glances, she'd stopped short of returning them until she was certain about her feeling for him.

To push herself at a man was not Jessie's way. The wise geisha who'd been her father's mistress had instructed the young Jessie in more than the mere mechanics of sex. She'd shaped the adolescent Jessie's attitudes toward the man-woman relationship, and had taught her to look on it as one of sharing. From those lessons, Jessie had learned that when the time and place were right, with mutual desire guiding both man and woman, there'd be no need either to offer or to ask.

When they'd dined together at Fort Chaplin, Jessie had seen the first signs that Joe Farnam was attracted to her, but for the moment had pushed aside her own stirrings. On such short acquaintance, it had been impossible for her to tell whether he was attracted to her specifically, or was simply responding reflexively to the needs of a man isolated from women for a long period of time. Today, his ready agreement to follow her suggestions, the manner in which she'd noticed Farnam gazing at her when he wasn't aware she was noticing, had helped her to make up her mind.

Stepping into the shelter of the cleft, Jessie spread the blankets from both bedrolls on the level sandy soil that formed its floor, and folded her poncho into a square, which she placed between the blankets. On the poncho she placed the food she took from Farnam's saddlebags: cloth-wrapped packages of sliced roast beef, a big chunk of cheese, and bread that the mess sergeant at the fort had provided for their meals. After completing these preparations for supper, she walked down to the river.

When Farnam returned, Jessie was in the water. She'd waded out and explored the shallows until she found a spot where there was a very light current and where, when she sat down, the water came up just below her shoulders. She was splashing the warm water over her bare shoulders when Joe Farnam rode back. He saw her from a distance, walked his horse down to the river's edge, and reined in.

"It looks to me like you've found the most comfortable spot in this valley," he said. "I envy you."

"Don't just envy me," Jessie told him. "The river's big enough for both of us. Come join me."

"I . . ." Farnam stopped short. With a note of hesitation in his voice, he said, "If you're sure you don't mind . . ."

"Of course I'm sure. I wouldn't have asked you, otherwise."

"Then I'll take your invitation."

Farnam swung out of the saddle and dropped the reins over the head of his mount; like all cavalry horses, it was trained to stand. Moving to place the horse between him and Jessie, he levered his feet out of his boots, and stripped off his light serge pants and gray flannel shirt. Folding the garments across the saddle, he hung his black campaign hat on the saddlehorn and started for the water, still wearing his balbriggans.

Jessie did not suggest that he take off his underwear, nor did she invite him to come and sit beside her. She watched Farnam cross the narrow strip of baked earth that lay betweeen him and the river's edge. He noticed her looking at him and turned aside as he waded into the shallow water, but not before Jessie had seen the bulge that had grown at his crotch. Farnam waded through the shallows, and when the water was knee-deep, he sat down a dozen feet from Jessie and turned to face her.

"I'm glad I took your invitation," he said across the ripples that separated them. "The water's fine, not at all cold. It certainly feels good after a day in the saddle."

"It looked so inviting that I couldn't resist it." Without appearing to do so, Jessie was watching Farnam, waiting for his initial embarassment to pass. She asked an innocuous question. "Did you find anything important when you looked around?"

"Nothing important, unless you count the signs I saw that this place must be used regularly."

"Do you think Ki and I read the signs right? That they were left by rustlers taking stolen herds into Mexico?"

"That's the only thing I can think of," he nodded.

"Didn't it occur to you that if rustlers can use this ford to move stolen cattle back and forth across the border, an army could use it to invade the United States?" she asked.

"Of course it did! That's one reason I don't understand why it isn't marked on our maps."

"I suppose that's something you'll have to wait to find out about until you get back to Fort Chaplin," she said thoughtfully.

Farnam nodded. His head was turned away as he studied the bank on the Mexican side of the river. Jessie decided the time for casual talk had ended. Without splashing the water, she stood up quietly, facing Farnam. He turned his gaze back from the far bank and saw her standing naked before him.

Jessie's arms were raised, her hands buried in her windtousled golden hair. The position drew her full breasts up to stand generously bold, and the faint breeze blowing caressingly across the stream pebbled their pink rosettes. Below her taut abdomen, her wet pubic curls glistened like dark honey as the water streamed over her hips and flowed down her perfect thighs.

71

Jessie looked directly at Farnam. He needed no other invitation. Rising from the water, he splashed across the short distance that separated them and took her in his arms.

Their lips met and Jessie opened her mouth to his tongue. She felt his erection pressing against her and slid a hand down, and for a moment while their tongues darted around, intertwining questingly, she stroked and squeezed him. Then she freed his pulsing shaft from the clinging wet balbriggans and guided it between her soft thighs.

Farnam's hands went to Jessie's full buttocks. He tried to lift her, to enter her, but she tightened her muscles and shook her head. Breaking their kiss, she whispered, "Not yet, Joe. The whole night's ahead of us. We don't have to be in a hurry."

"But I am in a hurry!" His voice in her ear was urgent. "I want you right now!"

"We'll enjoy one another more if we wait." With her warm, moist tongue, Jessie caressed Farnam's throat, lingering in the soft hollow between his chest and shoulder, where she felt the urgent pulsing of his blood just beneath his smooth skin. "Carry me to shore now, Joe. Let's go back to where I've spread our blankets. We'll be more comfortable there."

"I suppose you're right," Farnam agreed, his voice showing his reluctance to wait. Nevertheless, he began wading to the bank. "I just hate to let go of you, now that I've finally got you in my arms."

"I'll come back into them very willingly," Jessie promised, her voice soft.

Side by side, carrying their boots and with Farnam leading his horse, they walked the short distance across the sunbaked caliche to the break in the canyon's wall. Farnam put his horse in the cave with Jessie's, and came back out. They looked at one another across the blankets, the food for their supper laid out on the poncho between them.

Farnam indicated the packages of meat and cheese and bread and asked Jessie, "Are you hungry?"

"No. Not especially. Are you?"

"Only for you," he told her.

Letting his boots drop, Farnam reached for Jessie. She tossed her own boots aside and spread her arms, inviting him. Jessie pressed close to him, pushing her hips against him to bring back the erection Farnam had lost on coming out of the water. When the wet fabric of the undersuit pressed to her skin, Jessie shivered and began to release the long line of buttons that held the underwear closed from Farnam's throat to his crotch.

When Farnam felt her fingers working, he dropped his arms to let her strip the clammy garment off. Then he clasped her to him again, and his mouth covered hers while Jessie pulled the balbriggans down until their own wet weight dragged them to the ground. She cradled Farnam's sex in her warm hands, and then began stroking it gently to help it grow again.

They stood beside the blanket, holding their fervid embrace. Farnam became hard quickly under Jessie's caressing fingers, and as she felt him swelling and growing stiff, she also felt the gentle brushing of Farnam's fingertips through her damp pubic hair. He slid his hand between her thighs. She parted them enough to let his fingers rub gently along the soft lips that nestled between them. Then a fingertip slid into the warm nest that was quickly growing ready to accept him.

"Come into me now, Joe," Jessie invited when she felt the moisture beginning to form as Farnam's probing fingers moved within her. Her lips were on Farnam's ear as she spoke, and the warm breath that came from them was in itself a soft caress.

"Yes. Of course," Farnam whispered hoarsely.

Jessie sank back on the outspread blanket, pulling Farnam with her. They lay on their sides, their lips glued together, their darting tongues entwined. Jessie had not released her grasp on Farnam's erection. She bent her knee to open herself to him, and guided him as he raised his hips. She slid her lower leg under him and pulled her hips closer to him as the firm cylinder of flesh slid slowly in.

73

Farnam moved to bring his body above hers, but Jessie turned on her side and whispered, "In this position for now, Joe. Do you mind?"

Intent on entering her fully, Farnam did not reply, but shook his head. Jessie pressed her thighs hard against Farnam's hips, holding him in her shallowly, feeling his shaft throbbing to go deeper. She held him motionless for a moment, savoring the sensation. When she sensed Farnam's urgency mounting and felt him stir restlessly, she released the pressure of her thighs, spreading them wide and bringing her hips up to meet his as Farnam drove into her full-length.

Moaning softly with delight, Jessie lay quietly at first while Farnam pounded into her again and again. She knew he could not hold his fierce pace very long, and gradually brought her thighs together, forcing him to shorten his long, driving strokes. Lost in his own pleasure, Farnam did not at first realize that Jessie was controlling his rhythm, and when he did, he stopped and looked at her, his eyes worried.

"Am I hurting you?" he asked.

"No. I'm enjoying it as much as you are. I'm enjoying it so much that I want to help you last as long as possible."

"I'll go slower, then."

Jessie released the pressure of her thighs and let him go in deeply once more. His tempo slowed for a few moments, but soon he was racing again. Jessie did not move until she felt Farnam's muscles beginning to tighten. She waited until he'd buried himself in her at the end of a deep penetration, then locked her legs tightly around his waist and clamped him to her once more, holding him motionless.

"We don't have to hurry, Joe," she reminded him, her voice a soft sigh in his ear. "It's a long time until daylight."

"But don't you—" he began.

Jessie smothered his question by closing her lips over his and sliding her tongue into his mouth.

She held the kiss as she continued to savor the sensation of Farnam's hard shaft filling her. Her first response was building quickly now, and she did nothing to slow its arrival. After a few more moments she started to rotate her hips gently, rubbing the tip of her sensitive nubbin of erectile tissue against the fleshy cylinder that impaled her, until the first gentle spasm rippled through her body.

Farnam felt her shivering, and raised his head to look down at her. There was a question in his eyes, and Jessie shook her head before assuring him, "No. Not yet. That was just a beginning, not the end."

Farnam nodded. He rocked his hips from side to side while Jessie's shudders continued, and when they ended he lay quietly until she had relaxed and sighed contentedly. After a moment he began to caress her breasts with his lips, drawing their stiffening nipples into his mouth and teasing them with soft raspings of his tongue. Jessie arched her back as her muscles began responding to Farnam's flicking tongue. Then, dismayed, she felt him beginning to grow soft within her.

Moving quickly, Jessie used one of the geisha tricks her instructress had taught her. Slipping her hand along Farnam's belly, she slid it past the bond of flesh that still connected them. Finding the seam of flesh that started at the bottom of his buttocks and extended between his legs, she began to rub her tumbnail gently up and down along the little ridge, in a series of slow, prolonged caresses.

After a moment, Farnam's hips began to twitch. He moved his mouth to Jessie's, and thrust his tongue between her parted lips. He was still buried inside her, and Jessie felt him swelling again. She waited until he was fully erect, then wrapped her arms tightly around him and rolled on to her back, bringing him into the position he'd sought at the beginning of their embrace.

Farnam did not need to be urged. As soon as Jessie released the pressure of her thighs, he started driving. Jessie brought up her buttocks and clasped her hands in the crooks of her knees. Each time Farnam plunged into her, she yanked down on her knees and brought her buttocks up to meet his long swift thrusts. From the vigor of Farnam's strokes, she knew that he was close and she did not hold back. Farnam's chest began heaving, and between her

,thighs, Jessie could feel his body beginning to quiver.

Jessie herself was swept up in a whirlwind of sensation. She slid her hands down to her ankles and pulled them down to bring her hips still higher.

Jessie's entire body was tingling with painful ecstasy. She was aware of nothing but the pounding of Farnam's deep, penetrating lunges, then in mounting surges each nerve and muscle was galvanized into ecstatic pulsing life for a few glorious, electric moments as Farnam lunged for a last time before the hot spurting of his own climax filled her and he fell forward on her with a contented sigh.

They lay for a while suspended between awareness and deep lethargy as their bodies relaxed and taut nerves grew slack and the temptation to sleep became overwhelming.

Jessie pushed away the sleep-clouds. She was tempted for a moment to use the more esoteric arts her geisha mentor had taught her to bring Farnam erect again, but second thoughts told her that he was not mentally prepared to accept such attentions. She let herself relax fully, content to wait now, but aware that the rest of the night still stretched ahead.

Farnam brought her back to the present by stirring in her arms. He raised himself on his elbows and looked down at her. "You're a tremendous lot of woman, Jessie," he said feelingly. "Did I make you as happy as you made me?"

"Every bit," Jessie assured him. "And I know you will again later on, after we've rested."

Early darkness had crept quietly into the narrow canyon. The towering walls that formed its sides were black, the river invisible. Farnam looked up at the sky, dark blue in the east, with a few first stars showing now, shading in the west to an almost colorless blue, with a thin rim of sunset's last pink outlining the horizon.

"We'd better eat a bite while there's still enough light to see what we're doing," Farnam suggested. "The moon won't rise for another two hours, and even if we do have those few sticks of wood, it might not be wise to light a fire."

Jessie suddenly discovered that she was ravenously hungry. "A good idea," she replied. She smiled and added, "When I said a while ago that we had the whole night ahead of us, it didn't occur to me that nights can be short as well as long. And I've got a feeling now that this might be a night that won't last as long as we'd like it to."

Lying beside the still-sleeping Joe Farnam, Jessie stretched luxuriously. Only half awake, she did not open her eyes, but raised her arms above her head, arched her feet, and wriggled her bare toes. As she awakened fully and became aware that light was glowing through her eyelids, she opened her eyes to the dim light of early morning.

Beside her, Farnam stirred and opened his eyes. "I thought we were going to sleep late this morning," he said. "We sure didn't waste much time sleeping last night."

"You're not complaining, are you?" she asked.

"Of course not!"

"And I haven't said anything about getting up," she reminded him. "Ki won't be here for two or three hours, but if you feel like we just must get out of bed—"

Farnam cut her words off with a kiss. When they finally drew apart, he said, "I'd as soon stay here forever."

"Since we can't, do you think we ought to waste the time we've got left?" she asked teasingly.

Farnam answered her by bending over and nibbling with his lips at the sleep-slackened rosettes of Jessie's taut breasts. They budded under the gentle persuasion of his tongue, and when their tips thrust up firmly, he began to move his lips and tongue from one to the other before starting a trail of kisses up the cleft that divided the proud high mounds.

His lips progressed up Jessie's neck and across her chin until they were pressed to hers. As Farnam's tongue slid into her mouth, Jessie busied her hands on his rising erection, until his shaft stood stiffly ready. Farnam moved to roll closer to her, but Jessie put a hand on the light brown curls that covered his chest and pushed him gently back.

She rose above him on her knees, straddled his hips, and

leaned forward to let his tongue reach her breasts again while she took his erection and began rubbing its tip along the moist lips between her thighs. She kept up the gentle friction until Farnam stirred and tried to thrust upward to enter her. Then she slowly lowered her hips and slipped his rigid shaft into her.

For a few moments Jessie was content to crouch motionless above Farnam, revelling in the sensation of being filled. Then, raising her body erect, she ground down on Farnam's hips, as though to take him in even deeper, and began rocking her buttocks slowly on her lover's impaling sex.

Jessie kept up the rocking until her first light spasm seized her. She fell forward when she began to quiver, and sought Farnam's lips with hers. Their bodies pressed close, and they lay motionless, lost to the world, while the soft ripples of sensation that were flowing through Jessie's body faded and came to a halt.

Her voice soft, Jessie whispered into Farnam's ear, "I'll take you with me this time, Joe."

Pulling her knees up beside Farnam's hips, Jessie started rotating her hips. Sensation mounted quickly now, and soon she began to lift her hips high, until Farnam's swollen shaft almost left her, before dropping with the full weight of her body to take him in fully. Faster and faster she bounced above him. Farnam clamped his hands on her hipbones. He helped her raise herself up, then pulled her down quickly, their bodies meeting with a solid, fleshy *thwack*.

"Now, Joe, now!" Jessie panted as her senses began rioting. "Hurry! Faster!"

Farnam did not answer. He was panting into the throes of his own orgasm, thrusting his hips high, going deeper into Jessie than ever before, bringing her to a quivering, shaking orgasmic spasm as he lifted himself in one final upward thrust and began jetting as his body dropped back to the blankets. Jessie lay limp, sprawled on Farnam's lax body, and in the shaded recess of the cleft, they both fell into an exhausted sleep.

★

Chapter 8

Farnam's tensing muscles brought Jessie snapping into wakefulness. She was still lying on top of him, and he was still inside her, though now she could hardly feel the soft flesh that had been such a satisfyingly rigid rod when they'd gone to sleep. Jessie raised her head. Farnam's eyes were open, his neck twisted to one side as he craned to look out of the cleft across the valley floor.

"I'm sure some sort of noise woke me up," Farnam said.

"What kind of noise?"

"I don't know. All I know is that I woke up and heard something, a scraping of some kind. It hasn't sounded since."

"I guess I didn't hear it," Jessie frowned. She stood up, took the two or three short steps necessary to reach the opening of the cleft, and added quickly, "But I do now, even if it's still very faint. Hoofbeats, and they seem to be coming from the arroyo we came in by."

"Is it Ki coming back?" Farnam asked. He stood up and came to join her.

Jessie shook her head. "It's still much too early for Ki to be getting here." She glanced at the sun, just above the rim of the eastern valley wall, and added, "He'd have had to start from the south ford before daylight to get back so soon."

"We'll be able to see who it is soon enough," Farnam told her. "It's a rider, all right. The hoofbeats are getting louder every minute."

After she'd listened for a moment, Jessie said, "Whoever it is, he's not in any hurry."

Farnam cupped a hand around one ear and turned his head in the direction of the noise. He said, "There seems to be only one horse, but sounds can be very tricky in a place like this."

"From what we've found out about this canyon, I don't think we can expect him to be a friend."

"I'm sure by now that you and Ki were right about this place being a bandit trail," Farnam said. "My guess is that it's a scout the rustler gang's sent to prowl the range on this side of the border and locate another herd to steal."

"We'd better get some clothes on," Jessie said, suddenly aware of their nudity. "Go ahead and dress first, Joe. I'll keep a lookout while you're getting into your clothes."

"Just stay well back out of sight," Farnam cautioned her.

"I'll be careful, Joe. But just in case that rider gets too close and catches sight of us, hand me my Winchester. If he should see us in here, I don't imagine he'll ask any questions before he starts shooting. If that happens, I want to be the one to get off the first shot."

Taking the rifle Farnam handed her, Jessie levered a shell into the chamber. Then she stepped back up to the opening of the cleft, staying well back in the deep shade that shrouded its interior. She peered out just in time to see a lone horseman come from the arroyo and start along the far wall of the canyon at a slow walk, heading toward the river.

"Has he come in sight yet?" Farnam called in a half-whisper from the back of the cleft.

"He's just coming into the canyon. Hurry if you want to get a good look at him."

"I can't hurry much faster, Jessie. These damned balbriggans are still wet. They're all tangled up. I'm having trouble getting into them. Besides, we'd both better be just as still as we can. Any movement from in here might catch his eye."

As the man came abreast of the cleft, Jessie tried vainly to make out his features, but the sun was quartering his back, and the wide brim of his hat cast a deep shadow over his face. Strain as she might, Jessie could be sure of nothing except that the rider wore a short beard.

"How close is he now?" Farnam asked in a low voice. "Those hoofbeats sound pretty loud."

"He's just passing in front of us," Jessie replied. "But I can't tell whether he's Mexican or Anglo."

"How about his saddle gear?"

"It's just like any other, Joe. Plain saddle, plain roan mustang. He could be a cowhand or a bandit or even a preacher, for all I can see."

"Let me have a look," Farnam said, coming from the back of the cleft to stand beside Jessie. The rider was past them now, and all Farnam could see was his back. He studied the stranger for a moment and told Jessie, "Just as you said, that fellow could be anybody, but he's sure got a cavalryman's seat."

"How can you tell that?"

"Look at his back, straight as a ramrod. The angle he's carrying his elbows and knees. At West Point, I studied the pattern enough to recognize it anywhere. Everything about him says that at some time or other he was army-trained."

"Our army?"

Farnam shook his head. "It's hard to tell. He'd have had the same training in the Mexican cavalry. They got their basics from the French, but Napoleon based his training on what Frederick the Great did. The British did the same, and so did we."

They fell silent, watching the strange rider's back as he rode on to the river.

"I think he's heading for that ford Ki crossed yesterday," Jessie said.

"That's about the only thing that'd bring him into this canyon," Farnam agreed. "Which means just—" He stopped short. The stranger had reined in at the water's edge and was staring across the Rio Grande. He sat motionless for a moment or two, then drew his revolver and fired two shots in the air, paused a few seconds, and fired two more.

"He's not going across," Farnam said. "He's signaling."

"Rustlers across the river?"

"I imagine so. It's the only thing that makes sense." Farnam paused for a moment and then said, "We'd better get out of here in a hurry, Jessie. If we don't move fast, we'll be trapped in this canyon. Get your clothes on, quick!"

Almost before Jessie could turn around, they heard distant shouts from the Mexican side of the river. They turned back to look. On the opposite bank, a small band of horsemen, clumped so that it was impossible to count them quickly, had appeared and were riding toward the river.

"*Hola, amigos!*" the man on the U.S. side called. He was answered by a medley of shouts from the opposite shore.

"Damn it, I know that voice!" Farnam said. He turned back to the opening. Jessie followed him. The rider on their side of the stream had taken off his wide-brimmed hat and was waving it in greeting to the horsemen from Mexico, who were strung out in single file now, getting ready to ford the river. The first two riders were already in the stream. "That's Henderson down there! Sergeant Buell Henderson! My top kick! What the hell's he doing here? He's supposed to be on duty at the fort!"

Farnam started out of the cleft, but Jessie grabbed his arm and pulled him back.

"Don't be a fool, Joe!" she said curtly. "I count eleven men in that bunch crossing the river, and the first ones are in the middle of the stream right now. You'd be shot down before you got halfway to that man on the bank. If you want to do something about him, use your rifle!"

"No, Jessie. I don't want to kill Henderson. I want him alive, so I can bring him in front of a court-martial!"

"Then you'll have to figure a way to catch him some other time. Our best chance of getting out of here alive is to go right now, and I've got to put some clothes on first!"

"Hurry, then," Farnam urged. "I'll saddle the horses while you're dressing."

Jessie had never put on clothes as fast as she did now. In three minutes, she was ready to ride. When she went into the cave, she found that Farnam had saddled her horse and was just throwing his McClellan saddle across the back of his own mount. She tossed the saddlebags across her horse's rump and was waiting to lead the animal out of the cave before Farnam had tightened the cinches of his own saddle.

"We'll try to make a clean getaway," Farnam said. "If we can beat those Mexicans to the mouth of the arroyo, the two of us can bottle this canyon up until Ki shows up. Then you can ride to the fort and get a squad back here."

Jessie shook her head. "Your men at the fort couldn't get here in time. Once the rustlers find out they're cornered, they won't stay and fight, Joe. We'll have our hands full, just getting away ourselves."

"No!" Farnam snapped. "I can't let those outlaws go back to Mexico!"

"How can you stop them?"

"Wait a minute, Jessie," Farnam said. "I can see one way to handle this, and it's a way that ought to please you."

"What's the way?"

"We hide right here in the cave, and let that gang go out through the arroyo. If we're right about them being rustlers, they're heading for one of the ranches east of the river. While they're stealing the cattle they've come for, I'll have time to move a squad of my troopers up here. When the rustlers come back, the troopers will be in position to bottle up the whole gang."

"It sounds like a good plan, except for one thing."

"What's that?"

"Suppose the rustlers stay here the rest of the day? What if they don't move out until dark, or even until tomorrow? If they do anything more than just ride through the valley, they're sure to see us."

Farnam thought about this for a moment, then nodded slowly. "You're right, of course. If they stay here more than a few minutes, they'll see us, and with the odds what

83

they are against us . . . well, we'd be captured."

"You know what that means, as far as I'm concerned," Jessie pointed out.

"Yes. I'm afraid I do. Let's go, then, Jessie! We can still beat them to the arroyo!"

Though Jessie and Farnam mounted quickly and spurred out of the cleft within seconds of reaching their decision, they'd waited too long. All the rustlers had crossed the river by the time they burst into the open. Almost instantly, the outlaws began firing. A slug from their first volley tore into a hind leg of Farnam's horse, and the animal almost went down before they'd covered a dozen yards.

"Back inside, Jessie!" Farnam shouted over the reports of the rifles. "It's our only chance to hold them off!"

Jessie wheeled her mustang and got back into the safety of the fissure's stone walls before the lieutenant could turn his wounded mount. She slid from the saddle, grabbing her rifle from its saddle scabbard as she dismounted. Stopping only long enough to lead her horse back into the cave behind the fissure, she hurried to the front of the cleft. Farnam was still outside, and Jessie began firing as fast as she could work the lever of the Winchester, snapshooting rather than aiming, trying to distract the rustlers long enough to give him time to get inside.

Her first shot took down a horse. With her second slug she knocked one of the front riders out of his saddle. Farnam pulled up his horse in front of the cleft. He leaped from the saddle and bunched the reins behind the horse's ears while with his free hand he pushed its nose around, trying to wrestle his mount to the ground.

Like all cavalry horses, the animal was trained to lie prone and shield its rider. With a shrill protesting whinny, the wounded horse dropped on its side and lay quietly. Farnam slid his own rifle from its scabbard and crawled behind the horse. Dropping to her hands and knees, Jessie crawled out to join him.

When the first outlaw had fallen from his horse, the rest of the band started milling, confused by the unexpectedly fast and accurate shooting. As Jessie and Farnam kept up their gunfire, the rustlers started drawing back to the river.

Spurring their mounts, they galloped across the valley at a long oblique angle that took them to the same side of the high rock wall that was split by the cleft. Their new position gave them a line of fire parallel to the wall and exposed Jessie and the lieutenant, who found their cover now reduced to that provided by the hind legs of the prone horse.

Slugs from the bandits' rifles began tearing into the hard soil all around Jessie and Farnum, who wasted no time in crawfishing back into the cleft. The rustlers' gunfire stopped when they saw their targets scuttle to safety. In the protection of the vee, Jessie and Farnam took stock of their situation while they reloaded.

"It looks like we ran out of luck in a hurry," Farnam said grimly. "I'm sorry, Jessie. I made a bad tactical mistake. I guess I was confused." He hesitated a moment, then added, "I hate to confess this, Jessie, but I've never actually been under fire before."

"You didn't act like it. And even if you did have buck fever, it ought to be over by now."

"I suppose it is. But I must've done something wrong, and now we're in one hell of a fix."

"Things could be worse."

"I don't see how."

"We hurt them more than they hurt us," Jessie reminded him. She pointed out to the valley floor. The body of the man she'd shot lay sprawled between the cleft and the river. A few yards beyond the motionless figure, one of the attackers' horses limped aimlessly around. "If there were twelve of them before, there's one less to worry about now."

"Even at that, we've got a lot to worry about," he replied. "My horse is crippled, and I think it took another slug or two after I put it on the ground. We couldn't make a run for it now, even if we wanted to."

"They can't get to us as long as we stay in here, Joe," Jessie pointed out. "To do any effective shooting, they'll have to be out in front of us, where there isn't any cover. We'll be all right as long as our ammunition holds out."

"We'll make every shot count, then. How many shells have you got for your Winchester?"

"Two boxes in my saddlebags. And a box for my pistol."

"I've got the regulation fifty rounds for my Springfield, and twenty for my Colt," Farnam said. "Less what I've fired, of course. What we've got between us ought to buy us a pretty good breathing spell, though."

They were silent for a moment, listening to see if they could get an idea what their adversaries were doing. All they could hear from the direction of the river was an indistinguishable confusion of voices and the occasional grating or thudding of horses' hooves on the caliche soil.

"We've got to know what they're doing," Farnam said after several minutes had ticked away. "I'm going to take a look and find out."

Laying his rifle down, he stepped to the open front of the fissure and dropped to the ground; then, pushing himself forward, he peered around the edge of the stone wall.

"I think they're getting ready to rush us," he said over his shoulder. "They've mounted up, and they seem to be talking things over."

"They'd be fools if they didn't try an attack or two. But when they start this way, we'll be able to get in a few shots before they get opposite us."

"Sure," Farnam said absently, his eyes on their enemies. "It looks like they're stringing out, getting ready to ride."

"I'm ready, whenever they start. We'll have a chance for a few shots before they get in line with us and can shoot into the cleft here."

"Yes." Farnam backed into the fissure and stood up. His jaw set grimly, he said, "Just one thing, Jessie. Leave Buell Henderson to me. I want to be the one who shoots down that dirty traitor!"

"I don't blame you for feeling that way, Joe. And there'll be plenty of other targets for me. If you—" Jessie broke off as hooves thudding from the direction of the river warned them that their attackers were on the move. "We'd better get ready. Here they come!"

As the rustlers galloped to the attack, it was obvious that they were veteran fighters. They did not come as a group, but split their force. A half-dozen riders were spurring toward the fissure, and Jessie and Farnam began firing. At the first shots from the cleft, the attackers made use of Indian tactics. They dropped behind their horses, hooking a knee around their saddlehorns. Protected by the bodies of their mounts, the rustlers came on to the accompaniment of thudding hoofbeats.

"Hold your fire, Joe!" she said quickly. "They'll have to expose themselves when they start shooting!"

Almost before Jessie had finished speaking, the half-dozen rustlers were in front of the cleft. They did not raise their bodies above the backs of their horses, but fired from beneath the bellies of the galloping animals, using their revolvers. The fire they sent toward Jessie and Farnam was unaimed, but the angry whine of bullets singing above their heads and splatting into the wall of the cliff behind them forced the defenders to keep down.

Now the second wave swept past. They rode erect, confident that they'd catch Jessie and Farnam with empty magazines. The first shots fired by the pair caught the attackers by surprise. The rustlers scattered, only three of them holding to a course that brought them past the cleft. As Jessie and Farnam kept shooting without letup, the fire from the riders' pistols became scattered and ineffective. Finally the three rustlers that had persisted in the attack wheeled and galloped off.

Farnam had identified his traitorous sergeant in the second group. As the riders retreated, the lieutenant stood up and took careful aim. His shot knocked the turncoat sergeant from his horse and he fell to the ground, his arms and legs flailing as he hit and rolled over, and lay still.

"We did better than just hold our own this time," Farnam said with grim satisfaction. "At least I—"

A shot from the rustler band cut off his words. Farnam's

jaw dropped open, his face contorted with pain, and his body twisted as he slumped to the ground beside Jessie.

"Joe!" Jessie said urgently. "Joe!"

Farnam moved, trying to sit up. Blood was staining the sleeve of his gray shirt just below his left shoulder. His lips worked as he tried to reply, but only a few hoarse gasps came from his mouth at his first effort, while Jessie was moving to his side. Then he found his voice.

"I'm...all right," he said slowly. "I think I am, anyhow."

"Hold on to me," Jessie told him. "I'll get you inside and see how badly you're hurt."

Farnam shook his head. "I can make it myself."

In spite of his protest, Jessie helped him with an arm around his waist as he pushed himself erect, using his rifle as a lever. A few faltering steps took them into the shelter of the cleft. Jessie helped him to sit down and lean against the wall.

"It doesn't look too bad," she assured him.

"Doesn't hurt much either," he said. "Just have to get my wind back. Damn it, Jessie, a man ought to hurt when he's been shot!"

Jessie was unbuttoning Farnam's shirt while he spoke. She pulled the garment down, exposing his shoulder and upper arm. The bullet had caught him high, above the biceps, and passed through cleanly. Blood seeped slowly from the blue-rimmed holes the slug had made.

"You're right, it's not really bad," she said. She fished a bandanna out of the back pocket of her jeans. "I'll have you fixed up in no time."

Folding the oversized bandanna into a narrow strip, Jessie quickly bandaged the wound. Farnam winced as she pulled the improvised bandage tight, but did not complain. When she'd finished, she leaned back, sitting on her heels, and watched closely for a moment while the blood seeping from the bullet holes stained the white pattern of the bandanna, but did not spread. Farnam watched with her, his face showing more curiosity than concern.

"It'll be sore for a while," she warned him. "And it ought to be cleaned with carbolic <u>ac</u>id or something pretty soon. But it's not as bad as it could've been."

Farnam tried gingerly to bend his elbow and raise the wounded arm. He winced and gasped as the effort failed. Shaking his head, he said, "There's just one thing that bothers me."

"What's that?"

"How the devil am I going to handle a <u>r</u>ifle now? Damn it, Jessie, you can't stand off what's left of that gang alone!"

★

Chapter 9

"You can use your Colt, if you can't handle a rifle," Jessie reminded Farnam.

He looked chagrined. "I suppose I'm a pretty bad example of a cavalry trooper," he said. "Sooner or later, I'm sure I'd have remembered I've got a pistol, but thanks for reminding me." He started to get to his feet. Jessie moved to help him, but he waved her away. "Let me get up alone, Jessie. I want to show myself that I don't need a nursemaid."

"Nobody's suggested that you do," she said a bit tartly.

"I didn't mean to sound ungrateful," Farnam apologized. "I'm just angry with myself, and it spilled out on you."

"It's all right, Joe," she assured him. "Now we'd better get out where we can keep an eye on the rustlers. I don't think they'll let this one setback keep them from trying to kill us."

Cautiously they edged to the front of the cleft and peered toward the river. The rustlers had just started riding in their direction. In spite of the long range and their need to conserve ammunition, Jessie let off two closely spaced shots at them. The rifle fire did not discourage the outlaws. The only effect of the two shots was to cause them to begin galloping sooner than might have been the case if Jessie had not fired.

Jessie and Farnam dropped flat inside the cleft as the rustlers spurred their mounts. The riders did not swing behind the bodies of their horses this time. Erect in the saddle, they poured rifle slugs into the cleft as they galloped past. The best the two defenders could do was to let off a quickly aimed shot or two as the last of the attackers came abreast. By that time, though, the members of the gang who'd been the first to ride by had wheeled and were coming back.

"If they keep us under a steady fire, we're done for!" Farnam said, raising his voice to make himself heard over the constant barking of the rustlers' guns.

"All we can do is fight back!" Jessie replied, her eyes at her rifle sights as she swung the gun, trying to get in an aimed shot. She squeezed the trigger, but too late, the man at whom she'd been aiming swerved just as she fired.

Then, as the last of the riders swept past the cleft and the rustlers' fire slackened, the distant crack of a rifle sounded from the mouth of the valley. The last rider's horse stumbled and broke stride, but managed to continue toward the river, limping badly. Another shot from the distance followed the first, and hard on the heels of that one, a third report rang out.

"It's Ki!" Jessie cried. "He must've heard the shooting as he was coming through the arroyo, and hurried to help us!"

"Whether it's your man Ki or somebody else, they got here just in time," Farnam said.

Jessie leaped to her feet and stepped outside the fissure. The outlaws were not waiting to find out who fired the shots from the mouth of the valley. Knowing that even a single rifleman could keep them from passing through the narrow, twisting arroyo, they were galloping for the ford.

Jessie let off the last shot in the Winchester's magazine at the fleeing outlaws, but the slug missed. By the time she'd reloaded, the band was well on its way across the Rio Grande.

The valley floor was deserted except for three riderless horses, one of them lamed, and the bodies of Buell Henderson and one of the rustlers.

Jessie looked up the valley as Ki emerged from the arroyo and spurred his mount toward the cleft. She waved, and Ki waved back, kicking his horse to a gallop.

Farnam gave a deep sigh of relief. He said, "I don't know when I've been as glad to see somebody—just anybody who's on our side."

Ki was within shouting distance now. He called, "Are you all right, Jessie?"

"We're both all right," she replied. "Joe's got a bullet hole in his arm, but it's not a bad wound. I didn't get a scratch."

Reaching the cleft, Ki reined in and dismounted. "I heard shooting when I was halfway through the arroyo, but there wasn't any way I could gallop in there. Who was attacking you?"

"Rustlers, we're pretty sure," Jessie answered. "They must have had a time set to meet one of Joe's men from the fort." She pointed at Henderson's body. "That's him. Joe got him the first time they attacked us after we'd holed up in the cleft."

"And I'd better go take a look, to make absolutely sure it's Henderson," Farnam said. He started toward the body of the man he'd shot. Jessie and Ki followed him. Farnam said, "You don't have to come along, Jessie, if you'd rather not."

"I've seen dead men before, Joe. I'm as curious as you are to find out for sure whether it is one of your troopers."

They reached the sprawled corpse, which lay facedown, and Farnam leaned over to turn the body over so that he could get a good look at the man's face. His one good arm proved unequal to the task; Ki stepped up to help him, and when the unpleasant job was finished, Farnam looked at the broad tanned face and nodded.

"It's Henderson, all right. I knew I wasn't mistaken," he told them. "I can understand now why this place got left off our military maps. Henderson was responsible for most of the routine jobs, like making fresh copies of maps and records. It'd have been easy for him to do a thing like that. And until now, I had no suspicions at all that he was working with those rustlers."

All three of them jumped with surprise when the supposedly dead man let out a wheezy groan. They looked down to find Henderson's eyes open and fixed on them.

"Lieutenant," he wheezed. "Looks like you . . . caught up with me, didn't . . . you?"

"Yes. And you know what that means, Henderson. Prison."

"Not . . . for me," the sergeant gasped. "I . . . I'm done for. I seen . . . too many men die . . . to be wrong."

"I think he's right," Ki said in a half-whisper. "He must be still bleeding inside, and he's been lying here—how long has it been since he was shot?"

Farnam looked up at the sun. It was still midway to the zenith. "It seems like several hours, but it can't have been more than a half hour since I shot him."

"That's more than enough time for a man to bleed to death," Ki observed.

"Maybe you can get him to tell you how he got involved with the rustlers, where their headquarters are in Mexico, which ranch they plan to raid next, things like that," Jessie suggested. "Anything we can learn from him will be useful."

Farnam squatted down beside the dying Henderson. He said urgently, "Henderson. You heard what the lady said. Make up a little bit for the crimes you've committed by telling us whatever you can about that bunch of bandits you've been helping."

"Never did ride . . . with them Meskins, Lieutenant," the sergeant said, his voice thready. "Just told 'em . . . what the man paid me for . . . passing on to 'em. That's why I come here . . . this time."

"What man?" Farnam asked. "And what did you pass on?"

"Dude I met in saloon . . . at Laredo. Year or so ago. That was just before . . . you taken command." Henderson stopped as a fit of coughing seized him. "Told Meskins about . . . ranches."

"When they were gathering their cattle to drive to market? Things of that sort?" Farnam asked.

Henderson nodded feebly. "Never stole none...myself."

Jessie whispered, "Joe. Ask him where the rustlers' head-quarters is, in Mexico."

"Where'd your rustler friends come from across the river?" Farnam asked.

"Never did...rightly know. Ranch close to San Pedro...is all I ever...found out," the sergeant gasped.

"What's the name of the ranch? Or the owner?" Jessie asked quickly.

"Damn Mex names...can't remember," Henderson replied. "Trays...some kinda trays."

"Any other names you remember?" Jessie urged.

"Goose...goose man," he whispered. "All...men..." Henderson's voice faltered, and he coughed. A gush of blood poured from his mouth. He coughed again to clear his throat, and when he spoke, it was in a voice so faint that in order to hear, Farnam had to lean down with his ear only inches away from the dying man's mouth. Henderson gasped, "Don't blame...nobody else at Fort Chaplin...for what I done. It was...just me..." Another fit of coughing seized him. It ended with a final shudder, then his body sagged with the finality of death.

"I guess that's all we'll ever find out," Farnam said as he stood up, himself a bit unsteady on his feet.

"You go with Jessie to the cave," Ki said. "I'll do what must be done here. Will you want to take your man's body to the fort, or shall I bury him?"

"Better take him back," Farnam said. "I think my horse is dead, but I know one of those the rustlers left isn't wounded. I'm not sure about—"

"Joe," Jessie broke in, "Ki's competent to do what he's offered to do. If we're going to start back for the fort, you'd better rest a bit before we ride out."

Farnam did not protest. He let Jessie lead him back to the cleft, and sat leaning against the stone side of the fissure while she made sandwiches of the beef, cheese, and bread left from last night's dinner.

"One reason you're so weak is that we didn't have time

to eat a proper breakfast this morning," she said as they sat side by side.

"That we didn't, what with one thing and another," Farnam said, smiling.

Jessie smiled too, and took another bite from her sandwich. When she'd chewed and swallowed it, she asked him, "Do you know anything about the town your man mentioned before he died? San Pedro, he called it."

"I've never been there, Jessie."

"But it can't be very far from Fort Chaplin. From what Henderson said, he knew something about it."

"All I know about San Pedro is that it's about thirty miles on the other side of the river, which makes it nearly forty miles from the fort. Remember, Mexico's out of bounds for anybody in the U.S. Army. And don't remind me of Henderson. He probably broke regulations just as he broke the law."

"Surely you mut have heard something?"

"Not that I can recall. To tell you the truth, most of what Henderson said was just so much gibberish to me. I can't really believe what he said about some man in a saloon— a man he'd never seen before, whose name he didn't know—making an offer to bribe him to get information about the ranches around here. Didn't you find that hard to swallow?"

Knowing what she did about the cartel's method of operating, Jessie hadn't doubted Henderson's story for a moment. Whoever the man might have been, he'd undoubtedly found out all he needed to know about Henderson before making the offer. The thought of trying to explain this to Farnam defeated her, though.

"I don't suppose it's totally impossible, Joe. Cattle are big business around here—all over Texas, in fact. And there's more profit in selling cattle that are stolen than in selling those you've had to raise."

"Yes," he said thoughtfully. "I guess that's true."

"But I was asking you about San Pedro. You're sure you

can't remember anything about it that would help Ki and me?"

"You're not going there, I hope?"

"Of course we are. Just as soon as we get you back to the fort and make sure you're all right. Sergeant Henderson said the gang's headquarters is close to San Pedro, and I don't intend to stop until we find it."

"Jessie! Don't you know you're taking a big risk?"

"Everything's a risk, Joe."

"If you want to look at it that way, I suppose it is. But it'll be late in the day when we get to the fort. Surely you'll stay there tonight?"

Jessie looked at Farnam and smiled. "For a man with a bullet hole in his shoulder, you're very persuasive, Joe. All right. Ki and I will stay at the fort tonight, but we're going to start for San Pedro early tomorrow morning, and if you think you can persuade me differently, you'll find out you're wrong."

From a distance, San Pedro appeared to be a prosperous and thriving community. Jessie and Ki reined in beside the winding, rutted dirt road at the first shady spot they reached after they saw the twin towers of its church. For a moment they sat without speaking, welcoming the shade; the sun had beaten on them all day with unabated ferocity, though it was now declining.

They looked down into the saucerlike valley in which the town stood. The village was still three or four miles distant, and the massive bulk of the church loomed above the roofs of the smaller buildings around it. The church and its towers had been built from blocks quarried out of the light yellow stone formations they'd seen all along the road, bulging out of a thin layer of poor soil. The towers were topped with domes rather than spires, and surmounted by crosses.

The plaza was outlined by a half-dozen large buildings made from the same stone used in the church, and the

97

dwellings that radiated from the plaza looked like the small, compact houses typical of most of the small villages of northern Mexico.

"At least looks as though it's big enough to have a hotel," Jessie commented. "And a restaurant or two."

"And small enough to make inquiries easy," Ki said. "We may be able to find out this evening where the rustlers' hideout is. At least Henderson gave us a clue."

"Yes. When he talked about 'trays,' I thought right away that the ranch must be *tres* something or other—'three trees' or 'three streams' or 'three hills,' perhaps."

"With that much to go on, it shouldn't be too hard. But we won't find out by sitting here."

Ki toed his horse forward, and Jessie followed his example. They rode on, not hurrying, knowing they'd break their journey in the town that night.

It was only when they reached the town's outskirts that they saw that their view from the valley's rim had been an illusion. San Pedro was a ghost, a shell, the result of the wars, uprisings, guerrilla battles, and revolutions that had torn Mexico during the sixty or so years since it won its independence from Spain. The small core of the original settlement that outlined the plaza was an island of good buildings in a sea of near-ruins.

Poverty was apparent in the tumbledown *jacales,* many of them once solid middle-class houses, that made up the bulk of the town. A semblance of streets as they must at one time have been could be seen in the handsome two- and three-story buildings of dressed stone on the streets nearest the square.

Surrounding this core was a hodgepodge of crude huts made from flattened kerosene tins, barrel staves, scraps of lumber mixed with stone blocks and adobe bricks—any materials that would enclose a few square feet of space and form a semblance of a roof. Though they served as habitations, they could not really be called houses.

After they had gotten a close look at the few people on the streets, Jessie turned to Ki and commented, "Such a poor town, Ki! The people look as poverty-stricken as the houses. I'm not sure now that we'll find a hotel or even a restaurant here."

"There'll be a place to stay and eat. All we have to do is find it," Ki said. "The square would be the best place to look, don't you think?"

They rode on through the mean streets to the plaza, and as Ki had predicted, on the east side of the plaza, opposite the church, a hand-painted sign swinging from a wrought-iron bracket identified the two-story corner building as La Posada Mendoza.

"You see?" Ki pointed to the sign. "And it looks as though it might even be comfortable. I will go and see."

Leaving Jessie to hold the reins of both horses, Ki went into the hotel. A three-step stairway just inside the door took him into a tile-paved lobby, scantily furnished with a single divan and three chairs. A desk stood in one corner beside an arched doorway that led into a second room, only part of which was visible. The room beyond the arch was furnished with several long tables, each with four chairs on either side—the dining room, Ki thought. There was no one in sight in either room, but as Ki started to go into the dining room, a smiling man bustled through the arched doorway. He stopped short when he saw Ki, and the smile became a puzzled frown.

"Qué quiere usted, Señor?" he finally asked.

Though both Ki and Jessie had a fair command of Spanish, they'd found it to their advantage to use it only when vitally necessary to do so; in the Southwest and much of the West, Spanish was almost officially a second language.

"Do you speak English?" Ki asked.

"Of certainty, Señor. It is that you wish a room, no?"

"Two rooms," Ki replied. "And supper for two later on."

Looking around, his face puzzled, the man asked, "You are not alone, then?"

"There's a lady waiting outside. My . . . my employer."

"Ah, to be sure. Two magnificent rooms I have, over-looking the plaza. Or, if you wish more quietness, two equally fine chambers at the rear." He indicated a broad stairway at the side of the lobby. "Would you care to inspect them?"

Ki debated for only a few seconds; the chance was great that he was in San Pedro's only hotel, and if there was another, the odds were equally great that it would be no better than La Posada Mendoza. He shook his head. "It won't be necessary. You have a stable, I suppose, for our horses?"

"Indeed yes, even a courtyard in the rear for carriages," the man said. "But permit me. My name is Pierre Salazar. I am the proprietor of the *posada.*"

"I am Ki." Ki smiled inwardly as he watched Salazar's face when he heard the unusual name. The proprietor's eyebrows went up as he waited for the surname, then he regained his aplomb with a visible effort and bowed.

"Señor Ki."

"My employer is Miss Starbuck. I will suggest that she come in while I take the horses to your stable." Ki took a double eagle from his jeans and handed it to Salazar. "This will cover tonight's accommodations and our dinner, I'm sure."

Salazar bowed as he took the twenty-dollar gold piece. "Adequately, Señor Ki."

"We will settle accounts when we decide to leave."

Leaving Salazar bowing for the third time, Ki went out to tell Jessie of the arrangements he'd made. "It's better than I thought we'd find here. Go on in, Jessie. I'll bring up our gear after I take the horses to the stable."

When Ki came back into the lobby several minutes later, he was carrying a pair of saddlebags over each shoulder; in one hand he carried the saddle scabbard holding Jessie's rifle; in the other he held his own bulging scabbard, which had two compartments, one for his rifle, the other for his best teak *bo*. Ki shook his head at the offer of help. He said, "Just tell me where my room is, and when your dining room will be open."

"I have to Miss Starbuck explained the hours of service,"

Salazar replied. "And you will find the door of your room open; it adjoins that of your employer. The conveniences are at the end of the hallway."

Ki acknowledged the information with a nod, and went up the stairs. He found the open door, dropped his burdens on the mahogany four-poster that stood at one side of the room, and tapped on the door that he assumed connected with Jessie's. She opened it at once.

"This is much better than I'd expected, Ki." She looked around the square, high-ceilinged room. "And the dining room should serve something besides chili and tamales, since I gather from his name that the proprietor is at least part French."

"We'll have to see." Ki glanced out the window; the sun was setting in a red glow, an arc of its rim visible behind the church towers. "But while it's still daylight, I think it might be wise for me to go and look quickly at the town."

He was picking up Jessie's saddlebags and rifle as he spoke; he carried them into her room, and she followed him.

"Yes. That's a good idea." With a frown gathering on her face, she went on, "But be careful, Ki. If that sergeant was telling us the truth, San Pedro is very close to the rustlers' headquarters. We don't know anything about the gang, but if it's a cartel operation, someone here might know about us. And in a town this small, strangers are always noticed."

"Don't worry," Ki said. "I remember the precept of Tsai Tau, who said, 'When a lion enters a room, all eyes turn to loo,, but a fly crawling on the wall is noticed by none.' This evening, Jessie, I shall be the fly on the wall."

★
Chapter 10

Opening his saddlebags, Ki took out several small cloth-wrapped packages and laid them on the bed.

"I thought you were going to be a fly, not a hornet," she said, indicating the parcels.

Absorbed in unwrapping one of the bundles, Ki did not look up as he replied, "When a fly suddenly becomes a hornet, the one who is about to swat the fly is not prepared for it to sting."

He took a stack of a dozen *shuriken* from the bundle he held, and rewrapped the cloth around those remaining. The thin, palm-sized octagonal blades with razor-sharp edges made a stack less than an inch thick.

Picking up a thin leather sheath that lay in the heap of packages he'd laid on the bed, Ki slid the blades into it and strapped the sheath on his right forearm, near the elbow. The sheath was ingeniously made; a spring mechanism pressed against the flat blades and dropped one blade at a time into his hand when Ki snapped his arm down sharply.

Taking off the creased and worn leather jacket he had on, Ki felt the thin cord of the lead-tipped *surushin* that he wore as a belt. Satisfied that it had no frayed spots, he wrapped another *surushin* over it; this one had a thicker connecting line and heavier weights. The two *surushin* were almost hidden by the fold that Ki arranged in his shirt at the waist. Anyone giving his costume a casual glance would mistake them for a rope belt.

Now Ki unfolded a second bundle wrapped in a lightly oiled cloth, and from it took a few *shuriken* smaller than those in the sheath. These were star-shaped and no bigger than silver dollars. Ki dropped them into the side pocket of his shirt.

Patting his waist to give his shirt the proper drape, Ki took his *bo* from the carrying case that formed the odd bulge on the saddle scabbard that held his rifle. The *bo* was made from teak. Its wood had been soaked for a year in tung oil before the sides were planed to form the staff's octagonal shape and to taper it from a diameter of more than an inch in the center to three quarters of an inch at each end.

The artisan who'd fashioned the *bo* had sawed it into two sections of equal length and created an ingenious mechanism whereby one of the two ends could be affixed to the other and locked in place with a single twist.

As a final step, the *bo* had undergone a second year of soaking in light oil kept constantly warm, and allowed to dry in the hot sun for a final year to drive out the excess oil. Then, buffed and polished until its surface glowed, the *bo* was declared finished except for a final test. The test was to shatter a sword blade with one blow.

When Ki locked the two sections of the *bo* together, he held a staff five feet long. In the hands of an expert such as he'd made himself by long hours of rigorous training, the *bo* was a fearsome weapon indeed.

Though she'd seen Ki preparing for the unexpected many times in the past, Jessie still watched his meticulous movements with fascinated interest. When Ki took off his headband and picked up his *bo* she said, "While you're gone, I'll see if the conveniences here include a bathtub. You will be back in time for dinner, I suppose?"

"Of course." Ki pushed aside the hat he'd worn while he and Jessie were traveling, and took a plain black headband from his saddlebags; he knotted the band to hold his straight glossy hair in place. He'd noticed that a short man with a hat on his head feels taller than a taller, bareheaded man standing beside him.

After a moment's thought he also removed his sandals,

for another of his observations had been that a man wearing boots generally considers a barefoot man beneath his notice.

"I'll go out by the back door; it opens on the courtyard where the stables are," Ki told Jessie. "I've shocked Salazar enough for one day."

Jessie nodded. "I'll be in my room when you get back. Try not to stay too long, Ki. I'm already beginning to feel hungry."

Ki nodded and left. He went down the deserted backstairs and through the courtyard into the street. The sun had gone down now, and in the center of the plaza, beside a fountain long gone dry, torches had been lighted, their flames shedding a bright glare over the square. Beneath the torches, three men were setting up a table. Ki saw at a glance that they were obviously not *peónes,* even though they were doing what in Mexico was menial work delegated to servants.

All three of them, as well as a number of others lounging in front one of the half-dozen stone buildings that faced the plaza, were dressed in the *charro* style, in embroidered waist-length jackets worn over ruffled shirts, and trousers that fitted skin-tight from waist to knee, then flared out to the ankle. All of them wore wide-brimmed felt sombreros with high crowns, as well as crossed bandoliers studded with rifle ammunition. They all had on gunbelts with pistols, as well.

Around the plaza, people were gathering in little gossipy knots, and Ki smiled inwardly at the manner in which he and his clothing matched the local population. Most of the men wore simple cotton shirts and trousers similar to his, and while they were generally shod in *huaraches* of untanned leather, there were enough of them barefoot to keep Ki's bare feet from attracting attention.

Choosing an inconspicuous spot not too close to the table, yet near enough to hear what might be said, Ki hunkered down. He seemed to be leaning on his staff, but was always poised and ready to move. Almost at once he was surrounded by the pack of dogs that roamed the open area of the square. The pack was not aggressive, but it tended to attract unwanted noticed wherever it roamed.

Ki uttered a command. Though he spoke in Japanese, he used the *ninja* technique known as *ninpo inubue,* which made use of a tone of voice that animals instantly understood as representing irrefutable authority. They slunk quietly away and did not return.

A young Mexican standing close by who had observed the incident remarked, *"Conoces portarse bien los perros, amigo."*

Ki looked at the youth with a frown, and shook his head.

"You speak not the Spanish?" the young man asked.

Again Ki shook his head, but this time he said, "No. But your English is very good."

"I am to have it from the *escuela de la iglesia,* the priests, you understan'?" When Ki nodded, the young man went on, "I am say you know well how to make obey the dogs."

Ki nodded. Then, since the youth seemed to be a safe source of information, he said, "I have just come to San Pedro. What is drawing so many people to the square this evening?"

"This is the day of the month when the *rurales* they collect *la mordita.*"

Ki frowned. He understood the word *mordita;* it was one of those Spanish words with several meanings. Literally, it meant "bite"; colloquially, its meaning was extended to "bribe" or "payoff," but he'd never heard of a case where a day each month was set aside for the public exercise of this long-standing Mexican custom.

He asked the youth, "What is it, this *mordita?"*

"Los rurales," the young man replied, flicking a scornful, downturned thumb in the direction of the *charro*-clad group. "To them we pay a small bit from what each month we have earn."

"Why?" Ki asked, curious to learn the reason for the unusual collection.

"De cada razón o nada razón," the youth said bitterly, then remembered and went on, "The *rurales,* they are have

106

the power, and do as they wish. When the strong want a thing, they need no reason to take it."

Ki nodded. It was, he thought, the old story of might making right. The young Mexican's bitter words were true, at least in San Pedro: Those who held power needed to give no reason for their actions.

He glanced around; the plaza was rapidly filling up with people. Most of the men were dressed like Ki and the young Mexican standing next to him. A few of the men looked relatively prosperous, and wore American-style business suits with white shirts and neckties, and city-type shoes. Some of the few women in the crowd looked prosperous too, but most of them had on the voluminous dark skirts and shapeless blouses of *peón* women, and wore black *rebozos* draped over their heads.

"It looks like everyone in San Pedro is here," Ki said to his new acquaintance. "Do all the people in town pay?"

Glumly the youth nodded. *"Todos. Los ricos y los pobres."*

Ki did not ask the lad to translate, but asked, "You're going to pay too?"

"Naturalmente." Reaching into the pocket of his loose trousers, he pulled out three silver *pesos* and showed them to Ki. "For these three *pesos* I am work all month. Now I am have to give one *peso* to the *rurales*."

"I still don't understand why," Ki told the youth.

"Why? Because, *amigo,* I am wish to live." His voice was as matter-of-fact as though they were discussing the weather instead of life and death.

A flurry of activity at the door of the rambling stone house where the *rurales* stood around the door drew Ki's attention away from the strange revelations his companion had been making. He watched the building across the square.

Whoever the man was who'd just come out the door, he obviously held a position of importance, if his clothing could be taken as an indication. Ki studied the newest arrival with increasing interest.

107

Like the others, he was dressed *charro*-style, but with blatant differences. The tall cone-shaped crowns of the other men's *sombreros* were tan or brown; the newcomer's was creamy white and embroidered with silver. The suits worn by the rest of the *rurales* were in shades ranging from black to light brown and were embroidered in silk braid; the one the new arrival had on was a delicate shade of cream, and its embroidery was gold. He alone did not wear the crossed bandoliers that were almost an official uniform of the force, but he wore a pistol belt with twin holsters from which protruded pearl-handled Colts.

Without looking at the men clustered around the door, the resplendent *rurale* strode down the flight of low steps that led to the unpaved street, and started crossing the plaza to the table his men had placed there. Silently the *rurales* who'd been waiting fell in behind him. All of them carried rifles now, as well as the pistols in their belt holsters.

Ki took advantage of the moments while the *rurales* were in motion to ask his new acquaintance, "Who is the man wearing the fancy suit? The commander?"

"Sí. Es el Capitán Onofre Guzmán."

In Ki's brain a connection was completed. As Buell Henderson lay dying, he'd said something about a "goose man." It had made no sense at the time, but now what had been only an odd phrase became a name.

"This Captain Guzmán, has he been here long?"

A sneer in his words, the youth snapped, "Too long! He is come here six years ago from Vera Cruz."

Ki nodded as he got his first close look at Captain Guzmán's face. The *rurale* commander was short and swarthy, his face almost a cube. Heavy ridges of bone protruded over his eyes, the ridges made more prominent by thick, glossy eyebrows. In the recesses between the overhanging eyebrows and his high, square cheekbones, opaque black eyes glinted. His nose was almost flat, its nostrils flared. A full coal-black mustache did not hide his wide sensual lips, and his heavy jaw matched the rest of his square features. Guzmán looked every inch a barbaric and inhumane man.

108

Looking neither to the right or left, the *rurale* captain marched to the table and sat down. The men who'd accompanied him from the house stood a little away from the table in a rough semicircle. Almost at once, a line began to form as the people in the square shuffled slowly up to the table.

Ki could not believe at first that he was watching an entire town submit tamely to open extortion. Then a thought occurred to him. The *rurales* might be collecting taxes in behalf of the Mexican government, without the people understanding why they were paying.

"This money Guzman takes, is it a tax?" he asked the youth.

His companion shook his head. "No, *amigo*. Each year from the capital, *el Distrito Federal*, the soldiers come to take the government tax."

Ki's anger mounted as he watched the residents of San Pedro standing in line to give a share of their pitifully small earnings to the well-dressed and obviously well-fed *rurales*. At the same time that Ki was growing angrier by the second, he was also controlling the emotion rigidly. He reminded himself that he and Jessie had not come to Mexico to right wrongs, but to find the headquarters of a gang of rustlers and to find out if the cattle thieves were another arm of the octopus-like cartel.

After a few minutes had passed, the youth standing beside him shrugged and started for the end of the queue. He turned to say to Ki, *"Buena suerte, amigo*. If I do not go now and pay, tomorrow they come for me. *Hasta luego."*

Ki waved. He watched the young man join the line and start the slow shuffle up to the payoff table. Then, depressed by what he'd seen and heard, he started back to the hotel.

Something had been added to the courtyard behind La Posada Mendoza, Ki found when he entered it from the street. A one-horse landaulet, old but well kept, stood in front of the stable. The black-enameled wooden door panels of the carriage gleamed from a recent waxing, the glass panes above the doors and in its small oval windows glittered, the leather top had been freshly varnished, and its

109

harness had the soft, waxy patina of carefully tended leather.

In contrast, the driver who was curled up asleep on the high box seat wore the baggy shirt and trousers of San Pedro's common people. He did not wake up as Ki walked around the landaulet, inspecting it. After he'd admired the venerable carriage, Ki went up the backstairs and to his room. The connecting door was ajar, and from the next room Jessie called him.

"Ki? Are you back at last? I'm half starved."

"We'll go downstairs and eat, then. I'm hungry myself."

Jessie appeared in the doorway. She asked, "Did you learn anything that might help us?"

"Enough to know we've hit a trail. You remember the odd thing that Henderson said before he died?"

"I remember two odd phrases, Ki. One was 'goose man,' the other was 'all men.' Neither of them made any sense."

"One does, now. The commander of the *rurales* here, a man who looks as evil as he must be, is named Guzman."

"Guzman," Jessie repeated. "Yes, of course. Goose man, Guzman. It makes sense, Ki!"

"I thought so. I'll go out and ask more questions tomorrow. I came back because what I saw tonight was painful to watch."

"Tell me about it while we eat dinner, then. I'm hungry enough to eat almost anything right now."

When Jessie and Ki reached the lobby, Pierre Salazar was sitting at the desk outside the arched door that led to the dining room. Through the arch, they could see to their surprise that the tables were mostly occupied. Salazar jumped to his feet and came to meet them.

"Ah, Señorita Starbuck! You have come for dinner, of course. And for your manservant, there is a table in the kitchen."

"Thank you Mr. Salazar," Jessie said coolly, "But Ki will eat with me in the dining room."

For a moment the proprietor seemed almost to protest; Ki could almost see the mental shrug he gave as Salazar decided to humor the unpredictable whims that so often give trouble to hotelkeepers. Then Salazar bowed stiffly, and led them through the arch.

Except for one table, where a young woman sat alone, the chairs in the dining room were occupied. After a moment's hesitation, Salazar led them to the unfilled table.

"Dispensame, Señorita Lita, pero estos norteamericanos—" he began.

"No desasosiego, Pierre," the woman interrupted. *"Sera un oportunidad para usar mi inglés. Sienteles."*

Salazar turned to Jessie and said, "Señorita Starbuck, Señorita Adelita Mendoza has graciously consented to share her table with you. I will leave you to become better acquainted, while I inform the waiter that you are ready to be served."

When Salazar had gone, Jessie and Ki stood looking at the table, trying to decide whether to sit opposite their unexpected companion, or beside her. Adelita Mendoza settled the matter. She indicated the two chairs across from her.

"Please, sit down," she said. She waited until Ki had held Jessie's chair and taken the one next to her, and then, in excellent, almost unaccented English, she went on, "Don't be worried by Pierre. He has French blood, you understand, which makes him excitable. Now tell me, where in the United States do you live?"

"Not too far from here," Jessie replied. "A cattle ranch about forty miles east of the Rio Grande."

"Then we have something in common to begin with. My father also breeds cattle, though I doubt that they're the kind you have on your ranch, Miss—"

"Starbuck," Jessie said.

"I wasn't sure, after hearing Pierre say your name."

"What kind of cattle does your father breed, Miss Mendoza?" Ki asked.

"I used the word loosely," Adelita replied apologetically. "He breeds fighting bulls for our *corrida de toros.*"

Ki had been studying Adelita Mendoza while she talked.

111

She seemed to be in her mid-twenties. Her chin robbed her of a claim to true beauty; it was too long and narrow for the rest of her face. Her brow was high, an oval rising smoothly from coal-black eyebrows to equally black hair. Her eyes were large and strangely light, a violet-hued blue, set between long lashes. A thin, straight nose with flared nostrils dominated her face. Her cheekbones were high and thin, her lips a wide red gash, parting when she smiled or spoke to show small, perfect, and gleaming white teeth.

She had on a dress of light blue silk and a *rebozo* of white lace draped around her shoulders. Ki wondered if she'd pull the shawl up to cover her head when she went on the street, as did the women he'd seen in the plaza.

"They're not quite the same as beef cattle, I'm sure," Jessie smiled.

"No. Much more beautiful, of course. I always feel a bit sad when we ship a consignment to a *corrida*. You have seen our *corrida*, of course?"

Jessie shook her head, and Ki answered, "No. That's something I've missed."

"You must plan to attend one while you are in Mexico, then, Señor—" Adelita paused and then said, "I'm sorry, but I didn't hear your name when Pierre made the introductions."

"My name is Ki." When Adelita said nothing, and Ki saw that she was waiting for him to give his surname, he told her, "That's all the name I have, Miss Mendoza. Ki."

"Oh. I see," she said, though it was clear she did not. "But you are not from the United States, are you?"

"I am now. But I was born in Japan."

"Oh." Adelita was obviously embarrassed; speaking rapidly, she went on, "It is odd how the custom of names is different in different places. I have six names, and my father has nine. He only uses one, of course, and his last name is very seldom spoken, since everyone simply calls him Don Almendaro."

Jessie and Ki exchanged quick covert glances. After hav-

ing so recently realized that Buell Henderson had pronounced "Guzman" as *goose man*, they reached the same
conclusion almost simultaneously. Henderson's dying words,
all men, could well have been the beginning of "Almendaro."

★

Chapter 11

So brief was the exchange of glances between Jessie and Ki that Adelita Mendoza was not aware it had taken place. She chatted on, "When we moved to the ranch—I was a very small child, then—I remember my mother and father arguing whether he should name this hotel Almendaro or Mendoza. But, as you've seen, my father had his way. He usually does, of course."

"Do I understand that your father owns the hotel?" Jessie asked.

"No longer, Miss Starbuck," Adelita replied. "It was the Mendoza family home, you understand, before my father decided we should move to the ranch. I think my mother did not want to move, or to sell the home here in San Pedro, so father made it into this hotel. Pierre managed the hotel for him. Then, soon after my mother's death, my father sold it to Pierre."

"It must be pleasant at your ranch, though," Ki said, trying to keep the conversation on the topic of ranches until he had a chance to ask Adelita about a ranch with *tres* in its name.

Adelita grimaced. "Every day is the same. The same house, the same rooms, the same trees seen from the same windows."

Ki asked the question he really wanted to. "Your father has several other ranches, I suppose."

"Oh, he has much property, but we live at the Rancho Mendoza because it is nearest to San Pedro."

"And you never travel?" Jessie asked.

"Father dislikes travel, Miss Starbuck. When he transacts business with others, they come to him. And the only traveling I do is an occasional trip from the ranch to San Pedro. But as father doesn't approve of me riding horseback, I must make even that trip in our carriage, which is very old."

"Is that the landaulet I saw in the courtyard?" Ki asked.

"Yes. It is in good condition, but not very comfortable."

"Even if you don't travel, you must have quite a few interesting visitors at your ranch," Ki suggested.

Adelita shook her head. "No. Very few. Most of them are beyond my age and only interested in money. I enjoy most the season before the *corridas* begin, when the *toreros* come to test the bulls. They are . . . well, it is a time I enjoy." She looked at Ki as though seeing him for the first time, and her dark eyes seemed to become opaque for a moment. "The way you move, you remind me of some of the *toreros*, Ki."

"If that's a compliment, I thank you, Miss Mendoza," Ki said. "But bullfighting is something of which I know little."

They were interrupted by a very young waiter bringing their dinners. There were boned chicken breasts, a mildly spiced rice, and brown beans mashed into a thick paste seasoned with strips of large, mild red peppers. A tall pillar of thin tortillas, wrapped in a large napkin to keep them warm, took the place of bread.

Conversation languished while they ate. Efforts by both Jessie and Ki to begin a line of talk leading up to the information they wanted failed to draw more than a few words from Adelita. She seemed to have pulled into a shell after what they'd considered a promising beginning.

Jessie and Ki had worked as a team for so long that they could communicate by a look, a raised eyebrow, an imperceptible nod or headshake, the movement of a hand or even of a finger. They agreed by such signals not to push too hard for the information they were after. They'd learned nothing new when the waiter cleared away the dinner plates,

116

brought individual *flan* shells filled with a cinnamon-topped custard, and placed a silver pot of coffee on the table.

They had barely tasted the dessert when Salazar came in and whispered into Adelita's ear. She nodded and stood up.

"You will excuse me, please," she said. "I have a small duty to perform. Perhaps we can talk again at breakfast."

Jessie and Ki were seated with their backs to the arched door that led into the lobby. They watched Adelita until she was almost to the door, then returned to their dessert.

Jessie said, "Obviously the girl knows nothing about her father's business."

"I understand it's not the habit of Latin men to discuss business matters with the women of their families."

"I'm glad Alex wasn't that way. If he hadn't started teaching me about his business when I was young, the cartel would have swallowed all the Starbuck holdings by now."

"We should ask Salazar about the Mendoza ranches, Jessie," Ki suggested. "Perhaps you'd better do that tomorrow. He looks down his nose at servants, as I guess you've noticed."

"Yes. But I don't see why I should wait until tomorrow. We've almost finished, and he was here just a moment ago, so he must still be in the lobby. I'll ask him when we go upstairs."

Jessie glanced over her shoulder, into the lobby. When she did not turn her head back at once, Ki asked, "Do you see him?"

"No. I was looking at Adelita. Evidently her father tells her something about his business, because she was talking to a man twice her age, much too old to be a suitor or a sweetheart."

Ki turned to look, but saw no one.

Jessie said, "You missed them. They both walked away, right after the man handed Adelita something. I couldn't see clearly what it was, but I'm positive it wasn't a love note."

117

"A message to her father, I'd imagine," Ki said. "But if our suspicions are correct, Jessie, it might be something we'd be interested in. What did the man look like?"

"Stout. Not very tall. A rather coarse face, though I just got a glimpse of it. He was very well dressed, judging by the gold embroidery on his coat sleeve, which was about all I could see when he handed Adelita whatever it was he gave her."

"Ask Salazar about the man, when you talk to him, then."

"I will." Jessie pushed her chair back from the table. "We'd better go, Ki. We're the last ones here, and if we wait too long I might miss Salazar."

When they went into the lobby, though, it was deserted. They looked at the several doors that opened on the lobby, and Ki shook his head. "Salazar could be behind any of those doors, and I don't think we want to make too much of a point of asking him questions about Mendoza. Why not wait until breakfast?"

"No matter what we might find out, there isn't anything we can actually do tonight," Jessie agreed. "And after the past few nights, I'm going to enjoy that comfortable bed upstairs."

"So will I, after I soak off the dust that I picked up on the way here. We'll decide what to do at breakfast tomorrow, then, after you've talked to Salazar."

Ki was sleeping as soundly as he ever did when on a mission and in strange surroundings, but the almost inaudible scratching on his door brought him instantly awake and alert. He knew it could not be Jessie summoning him; she'd simply open the door between their rooms and call him. As was his habit, Ki had been sleeping naked. When the scratching was repeated, he draped his shirt over his shoulders and padded barefoot to the door that opened on the hallway.

His mouth close to the panel, he asked in a half-whisper, "Who is it?"

Adelita Mendoza's voice was pitched at the same low tone in which he'd spoken. She said, "Ki?"

"Yes."

"Won't you invite me in?"

Ki opened the door a crack. Adelita stood in the dimly lit corridor. She was wearing a loose, filmy white robe that billowed below the cloud of dark hair drifting over her shoulders. Ki opened the door wide enough for her to slip inside the room.

"I didn't dare say anything to you at dinner," she said. "I wasn't sure whether there was anything between you and Miss Starbuck. I'm still not sure, but I decided to find out."

Adelita was standing close enough to Ki for him to feel the warmth radiating from her body. He said, "There isn't anything between Jessie and me except deep friendship."

"I began to see that, just before Pierre came to tell me the man my father sent me here to meet was waiting for me. When I looked back in the dining room, you and Miss Starbuck were leaving the table, and I didn't want to talk to you in the lobby."

"You didn't come here to talk now," Ki said. "Did you, Adelita?"

"No. And please call me Lita, Ki. I won't feel that we're such strangers, if you do."

"Of course, Lita."

She went on, "I tried to give you a hint at dinner, when I told you that you remind me of the *toreros* who visit the ranch."

"I got the idea you were more than just friends with some of the bullfighters, but I didn't take that as an invitation."

"It wasn't, Ki. My being here now is one."

Lita slid her hands through the unbuttoned front of Ki's shirt and ran them lightly down his ribs. Ki took his cue from her move, and stroked her cheek softly with the back of his hand. He was moving his fingers down to caress the sensitive area that lay just under the smooth skin at the side of her neck when Lita grasped his wrist.

119

Pressing the palm of his hand to her lips, she began running the tip of her hot moist tongue in a circle around its center. Ki's hand was too heavily muscled for the caress to be effective, and when Lita did not feel it moving in response to her efforts, she took his fingers into her mouth one by one and began to lick and suck on them.

Ki recognized her signal, but ignored it. He slid his free hand along her shoulders and pushed the filmy material of her robe away from them. She shrugged and the robe slid down to fall in a heap on the floor. In the dim light that filtered in from the room's wide windows, Ki could now see the dark rosettes of her firm high breasts outlined against their creamy skin. He bent down to kiss them and Lita rose on tiptoe, arching her back to make the quivering globes easier for him to reach.

Ki drew one of her nipples into his mouth. Lita shuddered with a sharp inhalation. She released Ki's hand. He brought it down to find the twin to the breast he was caressing with his tongue, and began gently rolling its firm nipple between his steel-hard fingertips.

Lita's hands had moved to Ki's torso by now. She began to purr like a cat, a soft susurration rising from deep in her throat as her hands slid soft and warm over the firm muscles that bulged symmetrically on Ki's chest and biceps. Her hands reached his groin and found his sex, still almost flaccid. Lita wrapped her fingers around its supple length and squeezed gently, trying to bring it erect.

Ki did not wish to become hard yet, and he had learned long ago to control each muscle of his body, even those that in most men respond involuntarily to stimulus. He kept himself soft while Lita fondled him, and continued his own caresses to her firm perfumed breasts, moving his lips and tongue from one to the other. Lita's hands became more active. She began pumping rhythmically when her softer caresses failed. Ki still did not allow his erection to become complete, nor did he let his mouth touch any part of her body except her breasts.

Lita maintained her pumping efforts for several minutes,

while her own muscles grew taut and the tips of her breasts more sensitive. Then she let go of Ki's shaft and twisted away. He released her readily.

"Can't you get hard, Ki?" she asked.

"Of course. But we're not ready for that quite yet."

"Do you mean you can make yourself stay soft, and then grow hard whenever you want to?"

"Certainly."

Lita thought briefly, then asked, "And can you also make yourself stay hard as long as you want to?"

"Yes."

"Are you going to prove that to me, Ki?"

"Why, of course I am. Or isn't that something you enjoy?"

"What I enjoy most is to feel a man grow hard inside me."

"Most women do."

"You can do that for me, Ki?"

"Yes."

Lita was silent for a moment, then said, "I mean that I like to feel a man grow hard inside my mouth. Do you like to have a woman love you that way, Ki?"

"It's a very good way to begin," Ki told her.

"Let me begin, then!"

Lita pushed Ki's shirt off and began rubbing her face over his smooth chest. Like most Oriental men, Ki's only body hair was at his groin; his chest was as smooth as Lita's breasts. She rubbed her face over Ki's chest and stomach, her hands cradling his semi-erect shaft. Ki could no longer reach her breasts and he began stroking Lita's back and buttocks, but did not touch or seek to touch her sensitive spots.

After a moment she put her mouth to Ki's ear and whispered, "Carry me to the bed, Ki! I want to feel you get hard while I caress you!"

Ki lifted her, a light load for his powerful muscles, and carried her to the bed. For a few moments they lay side by side. Lita offered Ki her lips and they kissed, tongues entwining. Ki stroked her breasts and stomach, feeling her muscles ripple and grow taut as he rubbed. He ran his fingers gently through her dark pubic hair, but made no effort to slip his hands between her thighs. Lita's breathing grew fast and shallow, and she began to quiver. Then she twisted away from Ki and rose above him, kneeling, her legs straddling his.

Bending forward, her unbound hair falling to frame her face in a dark tent above Ki's hips, she ran her wet tongue along the length of his shaft several times before taking it into her mouth. For a long moment she held him without moving, then she began to work her tongue around as her head bobbed slowly back and forth.

Ki relaxed his control enough to let his erection begin. Lita shivered with pleasure as she felt him swell and start to grow firm. She drew him into her mouth as deeply as she could, and slowed the movements of her head to a more measured tempo.

Ki slid one foot between her wide-spread thighs and rubbed gently with his big toe. His constant exercise had made his toe almost as supple as his fingers. He could feel Lita's warm juices start to flow as he drew the tip of his toe along her sensitive bud.

After a few minutes, Lita began to squirm. She tried to clamp her thighs together to hold Ki's foot motionless, but with her knees spread as they were, her effort failed. She started moaning and moving her hips in a way that told Ki she was getting near a climax. He stopped the gentle massage and thrust his toe into her, holding the arch of his foot against her quivering button with just enough pressure to keep her on the brink of an orgasm without allowing it to begin.

Lita released him from her mouth and asked, "Do you like to come this way, Ki?"

Early in his maturity, Ki had lost the reluctance of the Oriental male to release himself when there was no possibility of begetting a child. He told Lita, "I enjoy it a great deal. But it's still much too soon. The greatest delight is to delay that final pleasure until these earlier ones have become unendurable. Let me give you a different pleasure now, so that we can continue to enjoy each other longer."

Ki did not wait for Lita's reply, but clasped her waist and lifted her, turning her above him in midair. He lowered her to lie atop him, and raised his head to spread her thighs apart. Lita gasped as Ki's tongue slid into her and its tip found the hardened button that his toe had already brought to sensitive life. Her lips closed again around Ki's erection as his tongue began rasping her with gentle firmness.

Already on the point of orgasm, Lita reached the stage of trembling ecstasy almost at once. Ki knew from the twitching of her body that she could not match his capacity for control, and did not try to delay her any longer. Lita forgot to keep caressing him as she reached her climax. Her urgent tongue stopped moving as she closed her mouth tightly around Ki's hard shaft while she shook and thrust her hips hard against his face, and Ki savored the warm salty flooding of her flowing juices.

He did not stop when her trembling ceased and she relaxed, but kept his tongue busy. He carried her into another orgasm before he moved his head away. When Lita had grown calm after her second spasm, her lips and tongue became busy again, and she was still trying to bring Ki to a climax when he lifted her for the second time and raised her high enough above him to force her to release him.

"No, Ki!" she cried. "I want to taste you coming before we stop! Let me have you again!"

"You will," he promised, swinging her around and lowering her to lie beside him. "You will, but it is still too soon."

Lita's muscles were water-soft now. Ki knelt above her and grasped one of her ankles in each hand. He spread her legs and pushed her ankles away from him, bending her knees until he could place the soles of her feet on each side of his chest. Her knees were above her waist, almost touch-

123

ing the bed, and her thighs were yawning open. Lita grasped Ki's objective at once. She reached down between their bodies and guided his jutting shaft into her.

Ki leaned slowly forward and Lita cried out with pleasure when she felt the fullness of his penetration. As Ki kept lowering his body, the weight of his chest forced Lita's knees lower and lower, and his hard shaft pushed ever more firmly against her already sensitive button.

"Ay, madre de Dios, Ki! Chingame prestamente!" Lita cried, reverting to her mother tongue in the near delirium of her ecstasy. She groaned happily, *"Es mas dentro de algún hombre he penetrado! De cual mas vete?"*

"Un poco," Ki replied, forcing himself down a bit further.

Lita wrapped her arms around Ki's neck and pulled herself up to find his lips with hers. Her back was arched now like a bow drawn full, and Ki began to thrust. He moved only his hips, and kept the full weight of his chest and shoulders on her feet. Lita's cries rose and fell as he drove into her.

Ki moved deliberately at first, and when Lita began to writhe and tremble under him, he increased the speed of his hard thrusts until she shrieked and flowed again. Ki did not stop. He brought her to another orgasm within a few minutes of the first, and then drove on until she came for the third time. Ki did not relax after Lita's third orgasm, but kept her on the threshold between pleasure and pain with slow, deliberate thrusts of his bulging shaft. When she began building to another orgasm, he was almost ready to release himself.

"Do you still want to taste me when I come?" he asked in a soft whisper.

"Oh, yes, Ki! Yes!"

"Then it's time now for you to have your wish."

With the same swift, graceful movements that marked his combats, Ki withdrew from Lita and turned to lie above her. She grabbed his shaft and he felt her hot lips close around it.

124

Lita's thighs were sprawled loosely, and Ki spread them still wider. He bent his head and found her swollen, tender button with the tip of his tongue. Lita moaned when she felt his touch, but did not interrupt the attention she was giving him.

When Ki finally released his rigid control and let Lita's busy tongue and lips bring him to his orgasm, he drew his own tongue with rasping force along her sex, and with a convulsive twisting of her hips she began to flow as Ki spurted and spurted again and yet again, until his rippling shudders ended and he was fully drained.

Minutes passed before Lita stirred under him, and when she did, Ki moved to lie beside her. She sighed softly and passed her hand along his body.

"None of the *toreros* I've known has ever exhausted me so pleasantly, Ki. Can I stay with you for a while?"

"Of course. Unless—"

"You are thinking that Pierre might find my room empty and say something to my father? Don't worry, Ki. My room is only a step or two down the hall, and Pierre will be discreet. And the night is still young."

"It is, of course. Sleep if you want to, Lita."

"I will, for a while. But if you should wake me up for us to have a *velade* before I must leave, it would not make me unhappy."

"Perhaps I will. We'll wait and see."

Ki was almost as exhausted as Lita by the long day he'd had, and the unexpected strenuous exertions of the past hour or so. Lita went to sleep at once, and a few minutes later Ki dropped into a deep slumber.

He woke with a start. The first brightening of the false dawn was creeping gray around the edges of the drawn curtains at the window. Lita still lay beside him, deep in an exhausted slumber. Ki's sure instincts told him that something must have roused him. He did not move, but concentrated on trying to remember what he'd heard in the few instants when he hung between sleep and awakening.

Before memory could return, Ki got his answer. Muffled

125

footsteps sounded in Jessie's room, but they were not in the same tempo with which Jessie walked.

Ki reached the connecting door in two long strides. He flung it open just as the door that led from her room to the hall was closing. Jessie was not in the room.

★

Chapter 12

In complete disregard of his nakedness, Ki ran into the hall. Pierre Salazar was halfway to the stairs. He turned and saw Ki and began to run. Ki was faster than the hotelkeeper. He overtook Salazar before he could start down the stairs, and rolled to trip him with a quick *shankutsu* move. Grasping Salazar's wrist, Ki levered himself to his feet, bringing his captive with him. Salazar's eyes were wide with fright. He stammered, but no words came out. Ki did not speak. He whirled Salazar around and bent his arm up between his shoulder blades. Then he pushed him along the hall, back to Jessie's room.

As soon as he'd closed the door, Ki demanded, "Where is Miss Starbuck?"

Salazar did not reply at once. Ki shifted the hand that was locked around Salazar's wrist, moving it up to sink his fingers and thumb into the pad of flesh at the base of the hotelman's thumb. Then he squeezed. Salazar winced and his face contorted with pain as Ki's steel-hard fingers dug into the sensitive mound and compressed the network of nerves that ran through its flesh. He still said nothing, and Ki added to the agony his grip was causing by bending Salazar's hand sharply backward.

"If you want to save your hand, tell me what happened to Miss Starbuck!" he gritted.

Salazar could hold out no longer. "The *rurales!*" he gasped. "Captain Guzman! He has taken her!"

"Taken her where?"

"*Ay!* Let go my hand, and I will tell you everything!"

"Tell me everything, and I'll let go of your hand!" Ki countered, bending Salazar's wrist still more sharply.

"He took her to the headquarters!" Salazar gasped.

"Arrested her? Why?"

"One does not ask Guzman why, when he arrests a person. I only know that he came in and ordered me to knock on Miss Starbuck's door, and to call her. He said if I called, she would not be suspicious. I did what he told me to. When she opened the door, he had his gun drawn, and threatened to shoot her if she spoke. She said nothing, as who would? Then he took her away."

"In her nightclothes?"

"No. He allowed her to dress."

"Did he have a warrant to arrest her?"

"I did not ask. In Mexico, the *rurales* need no warrant to seize someone, Señor Ki."

"You're sure he took her to the *rurale* headquarters? That building across the square?"

"Where else?"

Ki fell silent. Speedy action was imperative, but he needed time to dress. He brought up his free hand up to Salazar's neck and locked his thumb and fingertips like a set of claws into the brachial junction at the point where the neck and shoulder join. Its blood supply blocked, Salazar's brain no longer exercised control of his body. In a few seconds the hotelman slumped into a semiconscious state that would last for a half hour or more. Ki lowered the comatose man to the floor.

Back in his own room, he found Lita sitting up in bed, her eyes still half-veiled with sleep. She looked at him as he slid into his jeans and strapped the *shuriken* case to his forearm.

"Aren't you going to come back to bed?" she asked.

"I'd like to, but I don't have time." Ki's mind was racing, trying to make plans. He slipped on his shirt, and as he was buttoning it he suddenly saw a way out of his dilemma. He said, "I need your help, Lita."

"To do what?"

128

"To get out of San Pedro with Jessie."

"Ki, something's wrong. What is it?"

He did not answer for a moment; he was wrapping his *surushin* around his waist. Then he asked Lita, "Does your father have enough influence to keep Captain Guzman from causing trouble for you if you do something that will make Guzman very angry?"

"Guzman would not dare cause trouble for a Mendoza!"

"He's causing trouble for Jessie and me. He arrested her a few minutes ago."

"Buy why did he arrest Miss Starbuck?"

"Don't ask me why, Lita. I don't know." Ki realized that he was about to take a risk, but had already decided that the risk of trusting Lita was less than that of leaving Jessie in Guzman's hands a moment longer than was necessary. He went on, "You said last night that you were going back to your ranch this morning, didn't you?"

"Yes."

"Can you be ready to leave in a half hour?"

"I . . ." Lita seemed bewildered. "I suppose so."

"Will you take Jessie and me with you, at least part of the way?"

"Ki, I don't understand all this! What is going on?"

"I don't have time to explain everything to you now, Lita. But will you have your carriage ready to go, as I asked you to?"

"For you, this morning, I would do almost anything."

"Then do this, please. Gather up Jessie's things and mine. Put them in your carriage. Oh—you'll find Salazar in her room. He's unconscious. Don't try to revive him; he won't come to, no matter what you do."

"What does Pierre have to do with all this? Ki, Pierre—"

"I'll tell you later. Have your coachman saddle our horses and put them on a lead-rope behind the carriage. When I bring Jessie back here, be ready to start."

"How do you expect to get her away from the *rurales?*"

"Don't worry." Ki slid his arms into the sleeves of his

well-worn leather jacket and transferred to its pocket the small *shuriken* he'd put in the pocket of his shirt the evening before. He said, "I'll bring Jessie back."

"Ki, there are eighteen *rurales* in Guzman's company! You can't hope to—"

"Yes, I can, Lita." Ki took his teakwood *bo* from the corner where he'd leaned it when he came in the previous evening. "Will you do the things I mentioned, and be ready?"

"I still don't understand all this, but I promise you I'll do just what you asked me to."

"Thank you, Lita. I'll explain everything to you later."

Reaching the street, Ki moved with determination rather than speed. He crossed the plaza at a pace that would not draw the attention of the few early worshipers, mostly women, who were heading for the church to attend early mass. In spite of the hour, the doors of the stone building that housed the *rurale* headquarters were open. A knot of pistol-belted men in the *charro* garb that marked them as members of Guzman's company were clustered on the building's steps.

Ki hesitated only only enough to study the group of *rurales*. Then, gripping his *bo,* he moved across the plaza. He'd reached the street on which the *rurale* headquarters stood, but still had not crossed it, when three of the *rurales* on the steps detached themselves from their companions and started for the church. Ki did not know whether Guzman had given his men orders to watch for him, but he felt he could take no chances. The three *rurales* in the street were the first to feel the impact of his *bo*.

Almost without stopping, Ki dropped the first with an upward swing of the *bo* that caught the man under his chin and knocked him to the ground, unconscious. Even before the first man began to topple, Ki brought up the lowered end of the staff in an identical blow that stunned the next man in line. Continuing the smooth sweep of the *bo,* Ki laid out the last of the trio with a horizontal smash to his jaw.

None of the three *rurales* had time to reach for a gun or

to call a warning to their companions, who were clustered around the door of the headquarters. The *rurales* on the steps were crowding up to the doorway, their backs to the street, when Ki struck.

There were five of them. The first fell when Ki snapped the tip of the *bo* across the nape of his neck. He took out the next man with a continuation of the swipe that had accounted for the first. Ki changed tactics then, for, as the second man fell, he staggered into the three standing in front of him, closer to the door. They turned when the falling *rurale* hit them, and, as they moved, Ki slid his hands to a new grip on the *bo*.

Using it like a lance, he jabbed the man who he saw would be first to face him, thrusting the *bo*'s blunt tip into the vulnerable spot on the bridge of the nose where bone and gristle come together. The *bo*'s tip smashed into the cartilage, splintering the bones that formed the bridge of the *rurale*'s nose. The upward force of the stab sent a sharp sliver of bone from the man's nose into his brain, and he was dying as he fell.

Swiveling his body gracefully, Ki accounted for the fourth *rurale* with a stab that dug deeply enough into the man's solar plexus to split his diaphragm and start him tumbling down the low steps, gagging at the pain and gasping for breath.

As he swung his body to put its full weight behind the *bo*'s stabbing movement, Ki brought up his left foot up, extending it as it rose. The sole of his foot took the last *rurale* squarely in the ear. The smash ruptured the tympanum and swelled its inner cavity, pushing the ballooning tissues into the sensitive nerves that clustered around it.

Disoriented by the painful messages that the disordered nerves were pounding into his brain, the man yowled like an animal. Unable to hear his own cries, the *rurale* twirled in his tracks several times, getting entangled with the man whose diaphragm had been torn. Hopelessly entwined, the two fell to the top step and rolled down to the ground, their bodies writhing in agonizing convulsions while the animal cries of the deafened *rurale* echoed across the plaza.

Ki had no idea how many more *rurales* were inside the headquarters, but he knew the cries of pain that the injured men were uttering would empty the building. The front door swung inward. Ki slipped around it and opened it wide, concealing himself in the narrow triangle between the inside of the door and the jamb. He did not risk looking when he heard the clatter of booted feet begin ringing out on the stone-floored corridor.

Clasping his *bo* and holding it ready, he waited for the running *rurales* to pass the door, then swung it shut. There was a bolt on the inside. Ki threw it.

With the heavy door closed, the shouts of the unhurt *rurales* and the cries of those Ki had wounded were muted. Ki did not know which of the offices was Guzman's, so he started down the corridor, listening at each door. He'd almost reached the end when he heard the angry voice of a woman through the panels of one of the doors. Even though the words were muffled by the door, Ki recognized Jessie's voice. He tried the knob carefully, and found that the door was locked.

Drawing back his *bo,* Ki thrust with its tip at the thin wood of the upper panel. Thick as the panel was, the steel-hard tip of the *bo* splintered it, taking a strip of wood an inch or so wide from its center.

Ki freed his staff and looked quickly through the opening. He got a glimpse of Jessie, in profile. Her arms were pulled behind her, and her wrists were tied. She knelt on the floor beside a massive desk that stood in the center of the room. Her blouse had been ripped off her shoulders and her high breasts were thrusting forward against Guzman's thighs. The *rurale* leader was leaning against the desk, in front of her. One of Guzman's hands grasped Jessie's golden hair, pulling her head up. His trouser fly was open, and his darkly ruddy phallus, erect and swollen, was an inch from Jessie's face.

As Ki peered through the split in the panel, Guzman was just turning his head toward the door. He saw Ki's eyes and let go his grip on Jessie's hair. Pushing past her, he started for the door, drawing one of the twin Colts that hung from his pistol belt.

Guzman had taken one step toward the door before he reached for the Colt's pearl grips. By the time he had the pistol drawn, he'd taken a second step and was within the reach of Ki's *bo*.

Ki had acted faster than the *rurale*. At the first instant that Guzman started toward the door, Ki had sighted along the five-foot length of the teakwood staff, and at Guzman's second long stride, Ki struck with unerring accuracy.

He jabbed the *bo* forward through the slit he'd opened. The weapon's tip hit Guzman below the base of his now-drooping shaft, and tore through his trousers into his scrotum. Screaming in a high-pitched yowl, the *rurale* captain doubled up, dropping his revolver to the floor.

Ki knew his stabbing blow would incapacitate Guzman for several seconds. He used the *bo* as a lever, and cracked the door panel around the slit to open a hole large enough for him to slip a hand through. He slid back the bolt and shoved. The opening door pushed Guzman to one side. The *rurale* chief was still bending from the waist and too stunned from pain to realize what was happening.

Ki took the most vulnerable target the *rurale*'s doubled-up body offered—the tip of Guzman's hipbone, where the complex of inguinal nerves passes over the iliac crest. The tip of the *bo* ground nerves into bone, and Guzman's body flew erect in a spasm of pain greater than that which Ki's stab in the testicles had caused. As the *rurale*'s torso was rising, Ki whirled in another spin to create striking force, and dug his stiffened toes into the side of Guzman's neck, just below the jawbone. Guzman gave a spasmodic quiver, dropped to the floor, and lay still.

"I thought it was about time for you to get here," Jessie said coolly. She had risen to her feet and was leaning against the desk.

Ki took a *shuriken* from his pocket, and used its sharp edge to cut the ropes that bound her wrists. She rubbed her wrists to restore circulation in her hands, then she pulled her blouse up over her shoulders. Only one button remained, and she slid it through the buttonhole with a shrug.

"What's next?" she asked Ki.

"We get out of here, fast."

In the corridor there was a great hubbub. The *rurales* Ki had locked out at the front door were pounding at its sturdy panels and shouting loudly. From the stairway at the front of the hall, boot heels clattered as the *rurales* who'd been on the second floor of the headquarters building started to respond to the shouts of those outside.

"To the back door!" Ki snapped. "That way!"

They reached the end of the corridor. It ended at a blank wall, where another hallway ran into it at right angles. Looking both ways, Ki saw two doors. He had no way of knowing where either one led, but Jessie was holding his left arm and it was easier to swing her into a right-hand turn. They ran for the door. Ki opened it and saw an enclosed courtyard. On their left a pair of tall iron latticework gates stood open, and beyond them was the street. On the right was a row of stable doors, the heads of horses visible through the opened top halves. The horses gave Ki an idea.

"Wait!" he told Jessie.

Running to the stables, he sped along the row of doors, pulling open each one as he passed. At the end of the stalls, he turned and retraced his steps, rousting out the horses, until the courtyard was filled with milling animals. Shouting and waving his arms, Ki drove the horses through the wide gate and into the street, then he and Jessie ran after them.

As they followed the spooked horses into the plaza, a medley of angry shouts rose from the front of the headquarters building, where the *rurales* from the upstairs quarters were trying to aid those whom Ki had felled on the building's steps. The *rurales* started chasing the horses, ignoring Ki and Jessie.

In the courtyard of La Posada Mendoza, the landaulet was waiting. Adelita was pacing nervously beside it, and the coachman sat on the box seat, holding the reins.

As Ki and Jessie reached the landaulet, Adelita called, *"Francisco! Ándale! Vaminos al rancho!"*

She opened the door and Ki boosted her and Jessie inside. Before he was in himself, the coachman had slapped the reins on the back of his horse and the carriage was moving away. Ki looked back as they rounded the corner beside the church. A dozen *rurales* had come out of the headquarters and were standing there in a huddle, arms waving in excited argument. They paid no attention to the landaulet as it started along the dusty road that led to the Mendoza ranch.

★

Chapter 13

When the towers of San Pedro's church were out of sight and no *rurales* had appeared on the dusty road to pursue the swaying landaulet, Jessie and Ki felt more comfortable. Certain that his *bo* would not be needed, and because it was an inconvenience in the carriage, Ki collapsed it and replaced it in its case. Lita had said nothing since they'd left the hotel, but now she turned to Ki, her lips set in a firm determined line.

"You and Miss Starbuck are safe now, Ki," she told him. "It's time for you to give me the explanation you promised when you asked me to help you. What sort of trouble are you trying to escape, that the *rurales* should be after you?"

Ki called on the silent communication that he and Jessie had developed through long practice. With a tiny flick of one eyelid and an almost imperceptible nod, he let Jessie know that he'd prefer to have her answer Lita's question.

From the moment Jessie had seen the method Ki had arranged for their flight from San Pedro, she'd realized they would have to give Lita some kind of explanation for their troubles. She'd decided to gamble that if their suspicions were true, and Don Almendaro Mendoza was involved in the cartel, Lita would know nothing about that aspect of her father's life. Jessie had an answer ready, one that was truthful, even if not complete.

"We're after cattle thieves, Miss Mendoza," she said. "We had to come by ourselves because we couldn't get help from the United States Army, which has orders not to cross the border into Mexico. And we believe that Guzman and his *rurales* are working with the cattle rustlers."

Lita nodded slowly. "I'm sure Captain Guzman wouldn't turn his back on anything that brought him money. He's as greedy as he is evil. But why didn't he arrest Ki when he took you prisoner, Miss Starbuck?"

Jessie shrugged and answered Lita's question with one of her own. "Who knows what was in Guzman's mind? He had no reason to arrest me; Ki and I haven't broken any laws in Mexico. All I can think of is that Guzman was hoping to force me to make some kind of confession that would give him an excuse to arrest us both."

"From what I saw before I broke into Guzman's office, he was trying to force you to do more than confess," Ki put in.

"I've heard that in San Pedro, no woman feels safe from Guzman," Lita said thoughtfully. "And he has looked at me—" She stopped short, was silent a moment, then said, "Of course, my father's name protects me, even from a captain of *rurales*."

"You said your father and Guzman are friendly," Ki frowned.

"No," Lita corrected him quickly. "I said they have some small business arrangment between them. Even though Father does not speak of his business with me, I know that he has no greater liking for Guzman than I do."

"And Guzman knows this, I'm sure," Jessie said. "Do you think he might try to take me back by force?"

Lita shook her head. "He would not dare! Besides, we have more men on the ranch than Guzman has in his company of *rurales,* and there is also a room full of guns."

"Will they fight the *rurales?*" Ki asked quickly.

"Of course, if Father orders them to. But I am sure Guzman would not risk a fight. My father has many friends high in the government. A snap of his fingers and Guzman would be moved or his rank as captain taken from him."

Ki nodded. Lita's remark confirmed still further the suspicion he and Jessie had discussed, that Guzman and Mendoza were linked through the cartel. They'd seen cases before where, to further the cartel's schemes, the international cabal had used all forms of pressure from bribery to blackmail to force men who had little use for one another to work together.

Jessie saw that Lita was satisfied with the explanation she and Ki had given. To divert the conversation from what could quickly become dangerous ground, she asked Lita, "How far from here is your ranch, Miss Mendoza?"

"It is fifty kilometers," Lita replied.

"Nearly thirty miles," Ki frowned. "A long ride."

"In the carriage, yes," Lita agreed. "But we should be there in the middle of the afternoon."

"Would the carriage move faster if Ki and I lightened its load by riding our horses?" Jessie asked.

Lita shook her head. "No. But I don't blame you for preferring a horse to this old landaulet. If Father didn't object so strongly, I'd ride my mare to San Pedro. But would you please call me Lita, Miss Starbuck? Surely the adventure we're sharing is enough to let us put formality aside."

"Of course. And you must call me Jessie."

"Yes. We will have a chance to get better acquainted while we are at the ranch."

"How large is your ranch, Lita?" Jessie asked.

"Oh, quite a number of *hectares*. Several thousand, I'm sure. You must ask Father, if you want to know how many thousand."

"And your father would be the only one who knows about the other ranches your family owns?"

"Of course. Oh, I know their names—the Rancho Estrella in Tehuantepec, Rancho Manopla in Durango, Rancho Tres Cerros, the one closest to the Rancho Mendoza, here in Chihuahua. But I have not even visited all of them."

At Lita's mention of the Rancho Tres Cerros, Ki and Jessie exchanged another of their understanding glances. Don Almendaro's daughter had just given them the last clue they needed.

"Don't you even visit the one nearest here?" Jessie asked.

"Not anymore. We went there often when I was a young girl, but it's been years since Father has felt like spending any time there. He seldom visits Tres Cerros himself."

Ki looked out the coach window. They were crossing the top of a seemingly endless plateau to which they'd climbed soon after leaving the saucer in which San Pedro lay. It was rolling land, low hills and wide gentle vales, unlike the arid, barren strip along the Rio Grande. There were trees in scattered clumps, open range covered with grass that was thin, but adequate to sustain herds of moderate size.

"Is the country around the Tres Cerros ranch like this?" he asked, nodding through the window.

"Oh, no," Lita replied. She pointed to the southwest, and in that direction they could now see a lower and even wider plateau than the one they were crossing. Beyond the plateau, through the thin, clear air, they could see rising the rugged, barren slopes of the massive Sierra Madre. Lita went on, "Our Rancho Tres Cerros lies that way; it is in the foothills of the mountains. There is much less good land around it."

"Do you raise cattle there?" Jessie asked. When Lita nodded, Jessie went on, "The range there must be like it is on my own ranch in Texas."

Lita looked searchingly at Jessie and asked, "Tell me something, Jessie. You are young to be a widow, but you must have inherited your ranch from a husband now dead—"

Jessie broke in. "Not a husband, Lita. My father."

"Oh. I had not considered that. And you manage it alone?"

"With help from friends such as Ki, and others."

"Your men obey your orders readily?"

"Of course. But I seldom give orders. I make suggestions."

"I see. Of course, on your ranch you raise cattle; on the Rancho Mendoza, the *toros bravos* are bred."

140

"That shouldn't make a bit of difference," Jessie said. "But I've never been to a ranch where fighting bulls are bred. I wouldn't know how to compare it with the Circle Star."

"You will have a chance to, when we get there," Lita said.

Midafternoon brought them to the Rancho Mendoza. It stood in the shelter of a wide valley, and from the valley's rim they looked down on a complex of buildings—barns, corrals, sheds, small houses, even a miniature bullring—spread in a rough semicircle around a large two-story main house built of the ubiquitous yellow stone of the area. Both Jessie and Ki gasped when they first saw the establishment; it was like no ranch they'd seen before.

"It—it's certainly not like the Circle Star," Jessie commented. "Maybe there *is* a lot of difference between raising cattle and breeding fighting bulls."

"Father would know about that, Jessie. I don't, but you can ask him."

"I will, when I meet him."

Lita bounded out of the carriage without waiting for Jessie and Ki. She started for the door of the mansion, then remembered and waited while they alighted. The door swung open as they went up the broad flight of steps leading to it. As they went in, Ki got a glimpse of a white-clad youth standing behind the door, ready to close it. They'd gone only a few steps before another door opened and a tall, angular man stepped into the hall. Lita stopped, and so did Jessie and Ki. They did not need to wait for an introduction to realize that the man was Don Almendaro Mendoza.

"I am back, Father," Lita said. Her voice was meek and a bit worried.

"So I see," Don Almendaro told her. "I also see that you have brought guests with you."

"Yes, Father. May I present Miss Jessie Starbuck, who

141

owns a large ranch in the United States, and Ki—" Lita stopped, frowned, and then finished in a rush, "Ki works with Miss Starbuck on the ranch."

Ki saw at once where Lita had gotten most of her features. Except for her mouth, which was rounded and soft, her father's face was reflected in hers. They both had the same high forehead and overlong chin, but Don Almendaro's mouth was a thin, severe line. He wore a *charro* costume of fine gabardine, the jacket and flared legs of the trousers decorated with gold embroidery. He gazed at Jessie and Ki for a moment before turning back to Lita.

"Did you welcome your guests as our custom requires?" he asked. His voice was neither warm nor cold, approving nor disapproving; it was simply neutral.

"No, Father. I thought—"

"Then do so, please. They are your guests."

Lita hesitated for only a moment before she said to Jessie and Ki, "Welcome to the Rancho Mendoza. Our house is yours."

"You did that very well, Lita," Don Almendaro said, still in a voice that held no expression whatever. "Since you are the hostess for their visit, I suggest that you take Miss Starbuck to the guest room reserved for the impresarios of the *corrida*. I will have Manuel escort Ki to a suitable accommodation."

"But Father—" Lita began.

"Lita." Don Almendaro's voice was suddenly stern, almost to the point of harshness.

"Very well, Father," she said. "Jessie, please come with me. Ki will be taken care of by one of our house servants."

Jessie and Ki avoided consulting even by a covert glance, under Mendoza's sharp scrutiny. After Jessie had started down the hallway, following Lita, Don Almendaro looked at Ki with a frown. Ki met Mendoza's eyes and kept his own face expressionless. For several moments the *hacendado* scrutinized Ki, then, still without speaking, disappeared into the room from which he'd come. Ki waited, his

142

face inscrutable, until a man of middle age came up the hall to where he stood.

"Se llama Ki?" he asked.

"Ki, yes, I am Ki," Ki replied. In the hostile atmosphere Don Almendaro had created, Ki intended to keep to himself the fact that he had a working knowledge of Spanish. It was one of the few assets on which he and Jessie could count.

"You do not speak the Spanish?"

When Ki shook his head, the man motioned for him to follow, and started down the hall. The servant led him out the back door and into one of the two-story buildings that stood in an arc behind the house. Inside, Ki found it much like some of the frontier hotels in which he'd stayed; it had a large central open area with small rooms closely spaced on both floors. The servant opened the door of one of them and indicated with a quick gesture that it was to be Ki's.

"Momentito," he said, then shook his head and went on, "Quick I bring *su equipaje.*"

Ki examined his surroundings. The small, neat room was furnished with a bed, a table, chairs, a washstand. Ki had occupied much worse rooms in many of the hotels where he'd stopped during his travels.

Shrugging, he went to the bed and tested it with his hand. Then he stretched out and gazed at the ceiling, his expression unperturbed, but his mind working at top speed. He had arrived at no plan of action before the door swung open and Lita came in, followed by the servant carrying Ki's equipment.

Before she spoke to Ki, Lita told the house servant, *"Pone el equipaje ahí, y vuelve a la casa."* She waited until the man had placed Ki's saddlebags and rifle in the corner she'd indicated and left the room before she said, "Ki, I'm sorry Father's insulted you this way! I shouldn't have let him!"

Ki sat up. "You didn't know what he was going to do, Lita. And I can only be insulted if I allow myself to be."

"I've explained everything to him," she said. "That you

aren't Jessie's servant, but the manager of her ranch. He said he didn't intend to insult you, though I'm not sure about that."

"I'll be very comfortable here," Ki said. He didn't add that he'd also have more freedom to move about and ask questions than he would in the house, where her father could keep an eye on him.

"Just the same, it was not a hospitable thing for Father to do, and I've convinced him he was wrong. I'll have your things carried to the house during dinner. Here on the ranch we eat early, usually about sundown."

"Lita," Ki said, choosing his words carefully, "I want to stay where I am. But if I do that, your father will be the one who's insulted. Don't you see? By inviting me to move to the house, he's trying to apologize. If I stay here, I'll be rejecting his apology."

Lita thought for a moment, then smiled. "Your mind's more subtle than mine, Ki. Father will be furious, and it will serve him right!"

"Besides," Ki told her, "I'll be very comfortable here."

"As comfortable as you would be in the *hacienda,* I suppose," she agreed. "It's where the *toreros* stay during the season when they test the bulls. You saw the small bullring next to this building. It is not as big as the ones where the *corridas* are held, but is exactly like them in other ways."

"I'm not really very particular," Ki said. "As long as I have a place to wash—"

"I'll send Manuel back with water and towels," Lita said. "And he'll show you where the dining room is when dinner's ready. It'll be just a little while."

To Ki's surprise, dinner went off very well. Though Don Almendaro was stiff at the beginning of the meal, the thin-bodied red wine served mellowed him a bit, and by accident Ki had opened their conversation by asking his involuntary host a question about the fighting bulls bred on the Mendoza ranch. Though he'd picked the subject primarily to keep the table talk from a discussion of himself and Jessie, it was perhaps the only topic that would have caused the stiff-necked Mendoza to talk freely.

"We call our bulls *toros bravos*," Don Almendaro explained. "And they are not of the stock that produces animals slaughtered for food. They are as untamed as a wild beast, their horns as hard as ivory, with tips as sharp as needles. Their muscles are like bands of steel, and their hearts as stout as a lion's."

"But how do you train them to fight?" Ki asked.

"They need no training. Their instinct is to fight. Their only training is done by the *toreros* in the bullring, from the beginning of the *corrida* until it ends with the bull's death."

"I understand your daughter to say that you trained the bulls," Ki said.

"No, no. I am sure Adelita said nothing of training. She would have told you we *test* the bulls," Don Almendaro said.

"Yes, Father. That is what I said. Ki must have misunderstood," Lita put in, her voice artificially meek.

Before Ki could ask the question he was forming, Don Almendaro went on, "We test our bulls for courage only. They must charge without hesitating when they see a man with a *muleta,* a small cape like a flag, moving in front of them."

"What happens if they don't charge him?" Ki asked.

"They are slaughtered for beef at once," Mendoza said promptly. "You must understand that bulls of the *corrida* can only inherit their character, their courage. Here I have two bloodlines, Las Astas and Tierra Buena. Both have been bred in Spain for many centuries, and in their breeding, care has been taken to choose only the finest bulls for sires. My bulls move with the speed and agility of a deer, but have the strength and stamina of their own kind."

"I know very little of your sport—" Ki began.

Mendoza interrupted him. "No! A *corrida* is not sport, not a game! It is a test of skill, like a duel between two swordsmen of equal ability. It is a measuring of the instinct of ferocity bred in the bull, and of the bull's courage against the *torero*, who has not the bull's great strength, but pits his skill and courage against the animal's."

"An exhibition instead of a game, then?" Ki suggested.

"Perhaps. If the bull learns quickly, it can sometimes keep the *matador* from plunging his sword through its huge shoulder muscles and a tiny gap in the bones, no larger around than a teacup, through which the sword must pass to pierce its heart."

"And the bull has no other point where it's vulnerable?"

"No. There is no man living who can kill one of our bulls as long as it holds its head high. The muscles of its shoulders must be weakened by the *picador*'s spear and by the weighted darts the *banderillero* plants in the muscles."

"Really?" Ki asked, his interest aroused for the first time. "Not one other vulnerable point, you say?"

"Perhaps I overstated," Don Almendaro replied. "If the bull should by some accident be cowardly, a *peón* butchers it with a short, stiff knife thrust into the spine at the base of its skull, to sever the spinal cord. But that does not happen often, not to bulls of the kind we breed here."

Ki grunted thoughtfully. "In my land we have the art of *te*, which means 'hand.' Those who have the skill can very easily disable or kill a man using no weapons at all."

"I told you how Ki defeated eight or ten *rurales* who had guns, and he used no weapons but his little staff and his hands," Lita put in.

"A man is not one of our brave bulls, Adelita," Don Almendaro said reprovingly. He turned back to Ki and said, "No man without weapons could ever stand against one of our Tierra Buena or Las Astas bulls. To think he could is foolish!"

"Perhaps so," Ki nodded. "But it would be interesting, philosophically, of course, to see *te* used on your bulls."

"This is a thing you will never see, I'm sure," Don Almendaro said brusquely. "It would not be permitted."

"I suppose not," Ki agreed, "since the rules of your

exhibition are so narrow. Just the same, it would be interesting."

"You might find it so," Mendoza said curtly. He refilled his wineglass and stood up. "Now I wish to speak with you of something else. We will go into my office and leave the ladies to gossip. What I wish to discuss, I prefer to keep between the two of us, for the moment, at least."

Not sure quite what to expect, Ki followed Don Almendaro out of the dining room. He glanced over his shoulder as he went through the door. Jessie was watching him, her face composed except for small worry-lines at the corners of her eyes, and the message she was sending was as clear as though she were speaking:

Don't trust Mendoza! Whatever you do, be careful!

★

Chapter 14

Don Almendaro's office was a large room, furnished spartanly with four chairs, a large desk, and a tall walnut armoire. Its only decorations were a shield bearing what Ki supposed was the Mendoza family escutcheon on one wall, and a pair of basket-hilted rapiers crossed on another. The *hacendado* settled into the high-backed armchair behind the desk. He did not invite Ki to take one of the other chairs, but Ki did so, uninvited.

"I will come to the point at once," Mendoza said. "Adelita has told me that you believe Guzman will bring his *rurales* here to attack my ranch. I must assure you that you are mistaken. He would not dare to make such a move."

"You must have a good reason for thinking that, Don Almendaro," Ki replied. "I can't see why he'd hesitate. Obviously, Guzman thinks he has the power to do what he wants to do, as long as he has his men to back him up."

Before the rancher could reply, there was a knock at the door. Mendoza called, *"Entrese!"*

Ki recognized the man who entered as Eusebio, the *mayordomo* or manager of the household. He carried a folded paper. He said, *"Es mesaje de San Pedro."*

Don Almendaro extended his hand, and Eusebio gave him the paper and left the room. Without apologizing to Ki, the *hacendado* unfolded the paper and scanned it quickly. His expression did not change as he read the message, nor as he refolded it, put it aside, and returned his attention to Ki.

"Suppose you are right," he asked. "Let us say that Guzman risks attacking the Rancho Mendoza. Adelita has told me that you wounded him with your cane or staff. How seriously did you injure him?"

Ki thought of the *bo* thrusts he'd driven into Guzman's groin and testicles. "Seriously enough to keep him from riding horseback for several days."

"If that is the case, I will not worry about posting a lookout tonight to warn us of an attack."

"There's one possibility," Ki said. "If Guzman decides to send some of his men without leading them himself—"

Mendoza shook his head decisively. "No. Guzman would not do that. He must lead them himself, to show he is still able to command. It is that threat which allows him to terrorize San Pedro with so few men under him."

"You seem to be very well acquainted with Guzman, Don Almendaro."

"Lita has probably told you that I deal with him in some small matters. Guards for special shipments of bulls to their buyers, things of that sort. It is wise to be on good terms with the *rurales*. There are still armed bandits roaming Mexico, you understand, and it is to the *rurales* that we look for protection against them."

"But if Guzman should attack, you have enough men and guns to defend your ranch?" Ki asked.

"Of course. I will lead my loyal men against anyone who threatens the Rancho Mendoza."

Ki decided it was time to offer a gambit. He said, "You haven't asked me, Don Almendaro, but Miss Starbuck and I will be here only tonight and tomorrow. I'm sure your daughter has told you that we came to Mexico in search of cattle thieves, and we think we know now where their headquarters are located."

Ki's remark did not seem to upset Mendoza. He nodded as though he had little interest, and stood up, saying, "I will not keep you longer, then. Goodnight."

It was only as Ki was walking back down the hall to the dining room that he realized Mendoza had not addressed him by name at any time during their conversation.

Reaching the dining room, he found the double doors closed. He opened one and peered inside; the table had been cleared and Jessie and Lita were gone. Ki shrugged. Jessie would find her own way to see and talk with him later, he was sure. He returned to his quarters and, without undressing, anticipating Jessie's visit, he stretched out on the bed and mentally juggled plans and possibilities until he dozed. A shift in the balance of the bed woke him and he opened his eyes to see Lita sitting beside him. She wore the same flowing nightdress that she'd had on the previous night.

"Lita!" Li exclaimed. Then, knowing the answer before he spoke, he asked, "What are you doing here?"

"Jessie asked me to tell you that she will be walking in front of the *hacienda* just after sunrise tomorrow."

"Why didn't she come herself?"

"Because we decided it would be unwise for both of us to be away from the house at the same time." Lita ran her hand from Ki's cheek down his chest, and stopped at his crotch. "And I am still waiting for the *velada* we did not have this morning."

"You thought it was unwise for both you and Jessie to be away at once, but not unwise to leave her alone and come here?"

"Jessie and I understand one another, Ki." Lita's fingers were busy with the buttons of Ki's fly. "I am no longer jealous of her. Tonight I will enjoy even more feeling you grow hard."

She pulled Ki's trousers down, and stroked him with soft fingers. Ki reached up to caress her breasts, and Lita shrugged the nightgown off her shoulders to bare them to his hands. She was bending forward to take his shaft in her mouth when the door of the room burst open. Don Almendaro strode in, a revolver in his hand. Behind him came two men whom Ki had not seen before. They both carried shotguns. Before Ki could move, all three weapons were leveled at the bed.

With Lita pressing down on him, Ki could not move. Had he been alone in the bed, he knew he could have

151

handled them, for in a fraction of a second he saw the entire sequence of *te* moves that he would have made: a quick backward flip, a *nagashi* spin to kick up the muzzle of the shotgun held by the nearest man, and a strike to send the man crashing into Mendoza, who would reel into the second man. If Mendoza or the second man had fired, the first man's body would have been Ki's shield against a bullet from Mendoza's pistol and the pellets from the shotgun.

It would have been so simple, Ki thought, if Lita had not been in his way. As it was, he could only lay motionless.

Don Almendaro said harshly, *"Adelita! Cubri su verguenzo! Tu es zorra! Puta! Vete a su cuarto inmediatamente!"*

Silently, Lita rose, pulling her gown up over her shoulders.

"Don Almendaro—" Ki began.

"Callate, hijo de cabrón!" the *hacendado* snapped. Ki did not try to say anything more. Mendoza waited until Lita had left the room. "You will be punished, of course. The punishment will be death, but a simple death by a bullet is too easy for such as you. For the moment, I will leave you to worry your mind about the way you will die. When I have decided, I may tell you." To the two servants, he said, *"Tome este bastardo al sotano. Y guardele bien!"*

Ki found the cellar in which the servants locked him to be much darker than the night. Even after he'd closed his eyes for an extended period, when he reopened them he could not penetrate the blackness. He groped his way around the walls, and found them to be of stone, like the floor. Resigning himself to spending the immediate future in total darkness, Ki curled up on the cold stone floor. He lay quietly, thinking, until his body grew accustomed to the chill, then he went to sleep.

The rattling of the padlock that secured the door roused him. Ki had no idea how long he'd been imprisoned, but from the emptiness of his stomach he decided the morning must be well along. Ki kept his eyes shut tightly to keep from being blinded when the door was opened, but even

152

then his eyelids glowed red when the hinges creaked softly
and a man spoke.

"*Andele, hombre!*" the man called; Ki recognized the
voice as being that of the servant whom Don Almendaro
had placed in charge of his guards when he was captured.
The man went on, "*Vaminos. Quierete el patrón.*"

Standing up, Ki found that the chill of the cellar had
caused his muscles to grow cramped during his imprison-
ment. When he went out, he saw that the man who'd roused
him was accompanied by two others. All three carried shotguns, and Ki decided the odds were against him with his
reflexes slowed by muscle cramps. He let them march him
into the *hacienda,* and down the hall to the office where
he'd talked with Mendoza the evening before.

Don Almendaro was behind his desk, leaning against the
high back of his chair. His face was no longer contorted
with anger, as it had been the last time Ki saw him. One
glance at the black smoldering eyes that stared at him convinced Ki that he preferred Mendoza in a rage to Mendoza
in the mood of cold, pitiless hatred that his features now
displayed.

In a voice as cold as his face, the *hacendado* said, "For
shaming my house and violating my daughter, I have decided how you shall die."

Ki did not reply, but kept his face passively inscrutable.
His lack of reaction touched a spark to Mendoza's anger.
When he spoke again, the old man's voice was sharp-edged.

"A Mendoza does not soil his hands by punishing a
barefoot *peón,* even one who has dishonored our family's
good name," Don Almendaro went on. "I will not give you
the honor of killing you myself. But I have remembered
that you spoke last night of a way men kill in your country,
with their bare hands. What was the name you gave to this
supposed skill?"

"We call it *te.*" Ki replied. He was sure that he knew
what was in Mendoza's mind, but still he kept his face
expressionless.

"Since you have acted in a manner fit only for animals,

153

I have decided that an animal shall execute you. You will die on the horns of one of my brave bulls."

Ki did not move or blink, but kept staring impassively at the *hacendado* after hearing his death sentence pronounced. Mendoza stared in return, but Ki's patience proved greater.

"Have you nothing to say?" Don Almendaro asked at last. "No plea for mercy?"

Ki shook his head. "Nothing I could say would change your mind."

"Most certainly not!"

"I would like to ask you a question or two, though."

Mendoza hesitated momentarily, then nodded. "Ask your questions. I will decide whether or not to answer them."

As though inquiring the time of day, Ki asked, "I am to be allowed no weapons?"

"None. You boasted of this skill you call *te*. I am giving you the chance to prove the boasts were true."

"When I kill the bull, you will be angry. Do you plan to kill me then? Or will I go free?"

Mendoza replied unhesitatingly, "In the very unlikely event that you kill my brave bull, you will be released."

"I have your word as an *hidalgo* on this?"

"I give you my solemn promise," Mendoza agreed.

This time, too, he replied without hesitating, but Ki had caught a tinge of doubt in his voice.

When Ki said nothing more, Don Almendaro asked, "You have no more questions?"

Ki shook his head, then said, "I suppose I will meet the bull in a corral or enclosure? If we must chase each other—"

"I'm sure you have seen the small *plaza de toros* behind the *hacienda*, where the *toreros* watch my bulls being tested. It is there you will meet your fate."

"Or where your bull will meet his," Ki said calmly.

"Bah!" Mendoza snorted. "You cannot defeat one of my bulls with your bare hands! The bulls I breed have shoulders like the mountains, muscles of steel, horns sharper than the swords of the *matadores* who face them! You will be carried dead from the ring! No man can kill a Mendoza bull without a weapon! Even after the *cuadrillas* of the *matador* have done their work, when the bull is tired and its shoulders torn and bleeding, the man with the sword feels the sour bile of fear rise in his throat when he steps from behind the *barrera* and walks out to meet one of my bulls!"

"A pretty speech, Don Almendaro," Ki said levelly. "But you may have made it too soon. When do I kill your bull?"

Still angry, almost choking on his words, Mendoza replied, "At noon. I sent men to the pasture for the bull soon after daylight, but they will not return for another hour. And the bull must be allowed to rest after having been driven here."

"To be fair, I must be allowed to rest too," Ki pointed out. "And I have had no food since last night, while the bull has grazed freely. Certainly I must be fed too!"

"Sangre de la Virgen!" Don Almendaro exploded. "You reason like a Jesuit!" He stopped, clenched his teeth, and then went on in a more controlled tone, "I am not an unjust man. There is truth in what you say. I will not return you to the cellar, but to the room you were given. And I will have food sent you."

Mendoza lived up to his promise. The meal he sent Ki was a generous one, and Ki ate hungrily, but wisely. Then, to conserve his strength, confident that his skill and trained muscles would respond to the challenge ahead, he stretched out on the bed to rest before the servants arrived to escort him to the bullring. He was lying on his back, staring at the ceiling, when the door opened quietly and Lita slipped into the room.

"Lita!" Ki exclaimed. He sat up on the side of the bed. "Where's Jessie? What happened to her?"

"Father has confined her in a room, but she's perfectly all right. She told me to say you're not to worry about her."

"And your father?"

"He's gone to inspect the bull the men have just brought in, and to see that the *plazoleta de toros* is in order." Lita sat down beside Ki. "Is it true, Ki? Are you going to face a Mendoza bull with no weapons but your hands?"

"Yes."

"Madre de Dios, Ki! You cannot do this mad thing!"

"I don't have much choice," Ki pointed out.

"Ki, you must leave here at once!" Lita said urgently. "I will help you get away. The guard at your door is in love with my maid, and she has lured him away so that I can help you escape. Let me——"

"No, Lita," Ki broke in. "Don't worry about me. I'll kill the bull."

"You can't! Bulls bred for the *corrida* have an instinct to kill men! That is their breeding, their heart! The bull will kill you with the first toss of its horns!"

Ki shrugged. "That's a risk I take, of course. But it's too late to change what your father has planned. Go back to the house now, and wait. You'll see I'm right, later on."

"There won't be a later on, Ki." Lita's voice was sad. She stood up, then bent to kiss Ki on the lips. *"Vaya con Dios,* Ki. You were a wonderful lover. I will regret that we never did enjoy the *velada* we missed."

Ki watched Lita's back as she went through the door, leaving with him the finality of her farewell kiss. Ki smiled, then lay down and stretched out again for a final few minutes of relaxation. He was still lying there when the three guards came, all of them carrying shotguns, to take him to the bullring.

They did not escort him through the wide door that led to the seats that arose in tiers above the small circular arena, but to a small door that opened into a narrow tunnel below the seats. Mendoza stood at the entrance to the tunnel.

"I must be sure that you do not have a gun or a knife," he said.

Glad that the *hacendado* had been so specific about his weapons, Ki replied, "I have neither, Don Almendaro."

He opened his scuffed leather jacket and showed Men-

156

doza that under it he had no gunbelt. The *hacendado* glanced at the cord of the *surushin* that Ki wore instead of a belt, but did not think of it as a weapon. He pointed to Ki's feet, which were bare, and Ki pulled up the legs of his trousers to show that he had no knife strapped to the calf of his leg. He did not mention the large *shuriken* in their case strapped to his arm, or the smaller ones in his jacket pocket.

Don Almendaro nodded. He said slowly, "I can almost find it in my heart to pity you. Almost, but not quite." His voice hardening, he went on, "In the *corrida,* it is our custom for the bull to enter the ring first. Since you have not seen our *plaza,* I have decided that you may enter first, today. You will have a few moments to look around before you face the horns."

"How do I reach the ring?"

Mendoza pointed down the tunnel. "A door, there. Outside is a small space between the wall and a length of fence, the *barrera*. After you enter the ring, you will have two minutes in which to inspect it. I have stationed two riflemen on the rim of the arena. They will shoot you if you try to run or if you hide behind the *barrera* to escape the bull. Do you understand?"

"Quite clearly," Ki replied.

"Then may God have mercy on your soul!" Mendoza said. He walked out of the door and closed it behind him.

Ki heard the rasping of a lock being secured as soon as Don Almendaro had closed the door. He kicked high a few times, and did a leg-bend or two, working the stiffness from his muscles. Then he went through the tunnel and out the door Mendoza had indicated. He walked around the edge of the *barrera* and stood on the smoothly raked sand of the miniature bullring.

★

Chapter 15

As soon as he saw the size of the small circular enclosure, Ki relaxed. His only concern had been how fast the bull would be moving when they came together. Ki knew the anatomy and vulnerable nerve centers of humans, but was not as familiar with those of a fighting bull. He knew where and how hard to strike when administering the single *te* blow that would paralyze an opponent; he knew the blow would be equally effective on a man of his own size or one weighing a hundred pounds more. What Ki still had to determine was the effect of his blows on a heavily muscled animal ten times his own size and weighing nearly a ton.

He was reasonably sure that many blows to the same nerve centers would be required to dispatch the bull. The problem he'd foreseen was that each blow must be delivered within a fraction of an inch of the same spot. If the bull was moving at a relatively slow speed, Ki was confident that he could administer the required blows with perfect accuracy, but he knew that the difficulty of doing this would increase in proportion to the speed at which the animal was charging.

Ki's first quick glance at the bullring told him it was not more than sixty feet in diameter. Any full-grown bull that Ki had seen on the open range needed fifty feet to reach its full speed in charging.

Once he'd satisfied himself that the size of the ring would sharply limit the speed the bull could attain in a charge, Ki looked at the ring itself. The perimeter fence was made from timbers three inches thick; they were held in place by wide, thick iron straps, a greatly oversized version of the hoops that hold a barrel's staves together. The *barrera* was also made of massive timbers, and like the walls of the bullring, it bore the splintered scars of many places where it had been struck by the horns of the Mendoza bulls.

To test the footing, Ki took several steps into the ring. The sand covering was no more than three or four inches thick, raked smooth, and only lightly compacted. It gave with a springy feel under his bare feet, and did not seem treacherously soft enough to cause his feet to slip when he launched a jump or landed when completing one.

Looking up at the seats that rose in tiers above the sides of the ring, Ki saw Jessie. She was standing between Don Almendaro and Lita, and Lita was arguing with her father. Aware that the two minutes promised him were ticking away, Ki quickly scanned the remainder of the ring. He saw the two riflemen, and across the ring from the *barrera* was the wide gate in the fence through which he guessed the bull would soon emerge.

A metallic clicking reached Ki's sharp ears, warning him that the gate was about to be opened. He gave in to the temptation to display a bit of bravado to Mendoza. Turning his back on the gate, he made a sweeping bow to the *hacendado*.

At the lowest point of his bow, Ki heard the grating of the gate's hinges and the snorting of the bull as it came charging out at full speed. The pounding of its hooves on the packed sand allowed Ki to judge his timing. Just as Lita screamed a warning, Ki sprang straight up. As the black shape of the bull passed below him, he caught the animal's hump of shoulder muscle with a sideways chop of his steel-hard feet, and used the impetus given him by the blow to carry him past the animal's tail and land upright on the sand.

As Ki landed near the center of the ring, he heard behind him the crash of the bull's horns hitting the sturdy wall of the arena. Ki whirled and saw the bull head-on for the first time when it finished swinging its massive body around

160

after its collision with the thick boards that formed the ring's wall.

Only now did Ki realize that the description given him of the Mendoza *toros bravos* had been understated. The bull he faced was midnight-black; even its shining horns and deerlike hooves were ebony-hued. Its head was broad, with a massive swelling at the base of its outspread horns. Set in the huge head were eyes as black as the horns and hooves; except for a thin rim of white around them, they would have been invisible.

It was the bull's horns that Ki noted most carefully during the few seconds while the animal stood swinging its head from side to side. Ki guessed the bull was getting ready for another charge, and held himself in readiness while he examined its gleaming black horns.

They were as thick at the base as Ki's muscular forearm. Their spread was wider than his chest, and the horns tapered symmetrically in a forward arc to menacing points. The neck of the bull was short, and it bulged with taut muscles. Behind the neck was the muscular hump of which Don Almendaro had spoken. The mound of muscle rose like a hillock on top and tapered down the bull's shoulders to merge with the animal's surprisingly thin, almost spindly legs.

While Ki's quick eyes were noting the body formation of the bull and contrasting it with that of the range bulls with which he was familiar, the great black animal charged again. Unlike bulls Ki had observed on the range, it did not paw the ground or lower its head and snort threateningly before moving. One instant the bull was standing where it had stopped at the end of its turn away from the wall, and in the next second it had covered half the distance to where Ki stood waiting.

As quickly as the bull moved, Ki moved faster. He saw the bull beginning to turn its head to impale him on one of its horns, and rose straight into the air again. When the bull's head was passing below him, Ki's foot lashed out in

161

a kick that caught the muscle of the animal's neck on the side opposite the one he'd hit before. In the fraction of a second that his foot rested on the bull's neck, Ki flexed his knees and leaped. The jump carried him over the bull's body and he landed erect on the sand, only inches behind the still-moving bull.

Ki waited with his back to the bull, confidently expecting to hear a crash that would tell him the bull had hit the fence on the opposite side of the ring. When he did not hear the clash of horns on wood, his instinct told him to leap aside instantly. It was Ki's first lesson in the speed with which a bull bred for the ring can turn and charge. His leap carried him out of danger, but barely so. The needle-sharp tip of the bull's horns tore through the loose fabric of his shirt, and Ki felt the cold horn when its curve behind the tip brushed against his skin as the bull thundered past.

Knowing now how quickly the bull could turn, Ki whirled at once to face its next charge. The bull was already turning to come back at him, its legs bunched like those of a deer about to spring while it swung its massive head to one side in order to provide extra momentum that would pull its body around faster and in a tighter turn. Ki could see no sign that the two blows he'd administered with his hard feet had affected the bull in any way.

As quickly as he'd formed his strategy of attacking the bull by weakening its shoulder muscles until it dropped its huge head and gave him a clear blow to its neck, Ki changed his tactics.

When the bull's charge brought him within range of its horns, and the animal moved its head to one side to bring the swordlike tips of the horns in line with Ki's body, Ki feinted a move that would have sent him beyond reach of the horn aimed at him. The bull began to shift its head to spear Ki with the opposite tip.

In the instant when the bull's horns were centered, its head and Ki's chest exactly in line, Ki dropped into a compact ball and rolled toward the bull.

In the split second that passed before Ki touched its

glistering wet muzzle, the bull could not reverse the direction in which it had begun to move its head. It lowered the massive horns to butt at the swiftly rolling ball that Ki's body had become, but lowered them too late. The horns were past Ki. He was now in the small triangle between the bull's widespread front hooves and its lowered muzzle.

Safely behind the lethal horns now, Ki unrolled his body in the same fluid motion with which he'd folded it. When he stood erect, the bull's neck was even with Ki's chest, and as Ki rose, he raised his arms high, clasping his hands together and going on tiptoe to give him a valuable inch or two of added height.

His fingers locked together, the toughened heels of his palms a single entity, Ki focused every muscle in his body into his sinewy arms. He brought his locked hands down between the base of the bull's horns and the hump of shoulder muscle, on the single three-inch gap that left the bull's vertabrae vulnerable.

Ki's hands hit with crushing force. They struck the key point for which he'd aimed his blow with the impact of a sledgehammer. The bull had swung its head fully to one side now, and the spinal cord that ran through the channel in its vertabrae was stretched tight. Ki felt the bones of the spine crushing under his blow. Then, with a small wet-sounding pop, the bull's spinal cord snapped, cutting of the vital impulses from the animal's brain to its muscles.

Though the bull was dead the instant its spinal cord broke, the momentum of the charge it had begun carried its body forward for a few more seconds. Ki used those few seconds to jump backward, carrying his body away from the bull. He turned and looked just as the black beast's forelegs began to bend. The bull slowly leaned forward. Its hind legs were still pushing it, responding to the impulse transmitted from its brain a split second earlier. The pushing of its legs speeded the bull's collapse. Its back arched as the rear hooves tried to move its huge chest ahead. Under the driving of its hind legs, the animal's forelegs bent and buckled.

Its head sagging now, the bull lurched into an ungainly heap and toppled forward to the sand. Its eyes were still open and glaring, throwing out tiny spears of light from the high noon sun until their pupils were covered with the film of death.

Ki was facing the fighting bull when it crumpled and fell, and he did not look away from the carcass until he was sure the animal was dead. Then he turned toward the stands, where Don Almendaro and Jessie and Lita were watching. He saw that they'd risen to their feet. Lita was holding her father's arm, and the two were arguing. Ki extended his arms, his hands spread wide.

"Don Almendaro!" he called. "I have proved to you that I could do what you said was not possible! Now tell your riflemen that I am free, and I will leave your ranch!"

Don Almendaro glared down at Ki, and his arm moved upward. Jessie, standing beside him, grabbed the *hacendado*'s wrist, but he shook her hands away. He started down the tiers of seats to the wall of the bullring. As he jumped from one row of seats to the next, he pulled a heavy revolver from beneath his coat.

"Brujo! Bastardo!" he shouted. *"Hijo de puta!* You have blackened the fame of the Mendoza bulls.! What my brave bull could not do, I will do myself!" Bringing the pistol up, the enraged *hacendado* leveled it at Ki.

Ki had dropped his arms after his appeal to Mendoza. He had no time to free his *surushin*. Snapping his right forearm sharply downward, Ki clasped the *shuriken* that slid from its spring-loaded sheath into his hand. He saw Mendoza's finger on the trigger of his revolver and knew that if he threw the *shuriken* to cut into the *hacendado*'s arm, he could not stop that finger from tightening. Ki took the only alternative he had.

Before Don Almendaro could bring his pistol to bear on Ki, the star-shaped steel disc was singing through the air, its razor-sharp edges glittering in the bright noonday sunshine. The shining blade sliced into the *hacendado*'s right eye, smashed through the fragile frontal bone of his temple, and cut deeply into his brain. The revolver sagged from the dying man's hand and fell to sand of the bullring while Don Almendaro was crumpling in death.

Ki glanced quickly around the seats. Neither Jessie nor Lita nor the riflemen had moved. The *shuriken* had sailed so swiftly to its target that it had been almost invisible, a gleam flashing through the sunlit air. In a mere instant it reached its target and performed its deadly mission in total silence. Only Jessie understood what had happened. Lita and the two riflemen were still staring at Don Almendaro. They saw him drop his gun as he bent and lurched forward before he fell, but until a stream of blood began pouring from his head, they did not realize that he was dead.

Lita understood before the riflemen did. She stifled the small shocked scream that rose in her throat, stared for a fleeting second at Ki, who still stood in the ring beside the dead bull, then started toward her father. Jessie grabbed Lita's arm and stopped her. She leaned forward and began speaking. Ki could see her lips moving, but the distance between them was too great for him to hear what she was saying.

Lita's eyes were still fixed on her father's prone form, and she struggled to break away until Jessie slapped her sharply. Lita had her arm raised, ready to strike back, before the reality of the moment came home to her. She stopped struggling then, and just in time. The riflemen stationed to kill Ki if he should try to run from the bull had been standing watching, waiting for their *patrón* to stand up.

When the seconds passed and Don Almendaro continued to lie motionless, it dawned on the two marksmen that through the same form of black magic that had brought death to the brave bull, their master had been killed by the man standing in the bullring. They started to level their rifles.

Jessie spoke quickly to Lita, and Lita raised her voice in a quick command to stop the men from shooting.

165

"Perez! Aleman!" she called. *"No les tiran! Obedecen! Mi padre es muerte! Soy ahorita la dueña de la casa de Mendoza!"*

Slowly the men lowered their guns. They stared wide-eyed at Ki, who still stood calmly, his arms folded now, in the center of the bullring.

One of them called out, *"Señorita! El hombre en la plaza es brujo! Permiteme matele!"*

"No, Aleman! Vedate! Ahorita, tu y Perez dicen a la gente de la casa que he sucede. Dicen preparales el funeral."

Aleman said insistently, *"Pero el brujo, Señorita Adelita—"*

Lita cut him short. *"No tengo miedo del extranjero."* Then her inheritance from Don Almendaro showed in Lita's voice as she added curtly, *"Obedecen!"*

Slowly, with every movement showing their reluctance to leave Lita unprotected from the man they were sure had killed Don Almendaro by some witch's trick, the two men went to obey her command, to tell the ranch's people that their *patrón* was dead.

Lita waited until they had gone before saying to Ki, "Come up to the fence, Ki, where we can talk without shouting."

Ki did as she asked, and as he came closer, Jessie moved unobtrusively aside. Ki looked for hatred or disgust in Lita's face, and saw nothing except calmness. He said, "I'm sorry, Lita. I killed him only to save my life."

"You don't need to apologize to me, Ki, or feel sorry about killing my father." Lita's voice was as calm as her face. "While my mother was alive, he made her life unendurable, and he's done his best to make mine the same way since she died."

"I could see that you two didn't get along well..."

"Be truthful, Ki. I hated my father and he hated me. All the people on the *rancho* know it. Most of them served him out of fear, or because their families have been Mendoza servants for two or three generations."

166

"If that's the case, then——"

"It is," Lita interrupted. "If my father had been a man of honor, he could have kept his solemn oath and freed you after you killed the bull. He dishonored his oath, and earned his death. What more can I say to you, Ki?"

After a moment's thought, Ki replied, "Very little, I suppose. And now that things have happened as they did, perhaps it would be best if Jessie and I left at once."

Unexpectedly, Lita shook her head. "No, Ki. Jessie has told me that you suspect the Rancho Tres Cerros is being used by the cattle rustling gang you and she came to Mexico to find. Will you stay long enough for the two of you to ride to Tres Cerros with me, so that I can see for myself?"

"Of course, Lita. Jessie and I would have gone there with or without you, but you should go and see for yourself what the situation is."

"I intend to. And I intend to find out what the arrangement was that Father had with Guzman. My eyes are open wider than they ever were, Ki. And as long as I am responsible for the Mendoza interests, I intend to keep them open.

★

Chapter 16

They saw the dust cloud long before they could make out the identity of the rider. Ki, Jessie, and Lita were riding abreast in front of the three men who were left of the dozen Lita had taken from the Rancho Mendoza to clean out any corruption they might find at the Rancho Tres Cerros. It had not been a difficult job. The *mayordomo* of the Tres Cerros and all but two of the ranch hands had disappeared. So had all the ranch's records.

Lita was at a loss to understand why until Ki had taken a ride across the property. What he found confirmed the suspicions that had brought him and Jessie to Mexico. In a canyon at the edge of the ranch, he'd discovered the Box B market herd; about half the steers' brands had been changed to "B House" by using a running iron to add a wide inverted V at the top of the box. He'd driven two of the steers, one with the original brand and the other with the altered version, back to show Lita.

"My father was more than a dishonorable man," Lita had said bitterly. "He was dishonest as well, and I was too blind to see it. When you asked me about the parcel he sent me to get from Guzman the night we met, it did not occur to me that Guzman was sending my father his share of the *mordita* that had been collected from the people there. Now I am shamed again to find him a common thief, no better than those who stole the cattle!"

Jessie and Ki had agreed before leaving the Rancho Mendoza to avoid telling Lita of their more serious suspicion, that Don Almendaro had been an agent of the cartel, and had quite probably been acting in league with Captain Guzman and his corrupt *rurales* in other areas besides cattle theft.

"What I can't understand is how Mendoza got involved with the cartel," Ki had said to Jessie while they were discussing what they should do.

"Owning a great deal of land doesn't make a man rich, Ki. I wonder if his *toros bravos* might not have been his downfall. He'd have made a deal with the devil to get bulls from one of the famous breeders in Spain."

"That's a possibility," Ki agreed. "The cartel may have offered him some kind of deal like that as bait."

"I'm sure there's a lot more Lita will find out," Jessie had said. "But she'll learn about it in time, and she has enough sadness to bear right now. Lita won't take the path Don Almendaro did, I'm sure. The cartel can't offer her enough to make her put a fresh stain on the family name."

Now, within a half-dozen miles of the Rancho Mendoza, the dust cloud warned them that still more problems loomed ahead. No one rode that hard on a hot afternoon just to stir up a breeze.

Aleman spurred up from the rear to ride beside Lita. *"Es Raúl que viene. Hay apuros al rancho, no?"*

"Quiza que sí, quiza que no," Lita said. *"Descubrimos pronto a pronto."*

Raúl pulled up beside them and touched the brim of his hat to Lita. *"Señorita!"* he gasped. *"Guzman y su rurales vienen al rancho!"*

"Cómo conoces?" Lita asked. She was as calm as though she'd just been told that it might rain soon.

"De mi primo. Llegarse a media hora, y digame."

"Cuándo viene Guzman?" Lita asked, still unperturbed.

"Sale de San Pedro en la mañana," Raúl replied.

"Bueno," Lita told the man. *"Estamos de vueltan prontito y decederamos que hace."*

When Raúl had dropped back to ride with Aleman and the other men, Lita said to Ki and Jessie, "You understood, of course?"

"Yes," Ki said. "Guzman's moved earlier than I thought he could. I really didn't expect him to show up so soon."

"You expected him, Ki?"

Jessie joined their conversation. "Of course, Lita. That's why we hurried so to wind things up at Tres Cerros."

"You might have told me," Lita said reproachfully.

"You'd just have had one more thing to worry about," Jessie replied. "And we couldn't be sure Guzman could organize an attack, considering the condition they were in."

Ki said, "At least he's not leaving San Pedro until tomorrow morning. That'll give us time to get his reception ready."

"We've done everything I can think of, Lita," Ki said.

He and Lita were standing on the roof of the main house, looking along the winding road from San Pedro. Less than a half hour had passed since one of the lookouts posted to watch the road from town had galloped in to report that Guzman and his *rurales* were nearing the sentry post.

Ki had estimated that the attackers would cover the distance in about the same time the lookout had required. He and Lita had now been watching for ten or fifteen minutes, so unless his judgment was bad, the *rurales* should appear very soon. He looked again at the sun, low now on the jagged western horizon, and still there was no sign of Guzman and his *rurales*.

"I still wish we had more men," Lita said nervously. "If we just hadn't left those hands at Tres Cerros, we'd be in much better shape to stand off Guzman."

"We'll hold our own with the men we have, Lita," Ki assured her. "We've got the advantage, even with so few men, because we'll be in the house and the *rurales* will be exposed. This house is built just like a fort."

"Ki's right, Lita," Jessie said, emerging from the trapdoor that led to the attic. "As long as your men follow orders and don't expose themselves when they're shooting. Rifle and revolver bullets won't go through these stone walls."

171

Before Lita could reply, they saw the dust. Ki frowned when he saw how slowly the cloud above the road was advancing. A band of riders should be moving much more swiftly. He tried to pierce the dust cloud with his eyes when through the dust he could see the first line of the *rurales*, but there had been no rain for months, and the cloud that hung over the approaching horsemen was too thick for even his sharp eyes to penetrate.

"There's something wrong," he told Lita. "Guzman might have a trick up his sleeve that we don't know about."

"What kind of trick, Ki?"

"I can't even guess. But I'm not impatient. We'll find out soon enough, and when we know what it is, we'll find a way to stop him from using it."

While they were still well out of rifle range, the *rurales* halted. The day was totally windless, and the cloud of dust the attackers had raised was slow to settle. The trio on the roof grew more and more impatient as they strained to try to penetrate the settling cloud. It dissipated at last, and when Ki saw what it had hidden, his confidence almost evaporated.

From some source known only to himself, Guzman had managed to get a cannon. Ki squinted through the diminishing dust cloud at the artillery piece. It was very old, so old that it might have come out of some military museum, and very small. Its barrel was brass, mounted on a low-slung wooden undercarriage. The *rurales* had loaded the ancient fieldpiece on an open wagon to transport it to the Rancho Mendoza, and were now setting long wooden planks at the rear of the wagon bed, preparing to unload the weapon.

In spite of its antiquity and small size, the cannon was an unexpected threat, one that Ki had not counted on when making plans to defend the *hacienda*.

"Guzman's given us an unpleasant surprise," he told the women. "That cannon changes all the plans I've made."

"Ki, it's such an old cannon, and so little!" Jessie protested. "Surely it can't make all that much difference!"

172

"It's not much of a cannon," Ki agreed. "But small and old as it is, it's got more range than our rifles. If we let him get that cannon into action, he can knock down this house and all the buildings around it while his men stay out of range until it's time for them to ride in and wipe us up."

"Surely such a small gun can't break down the stone walls of the *hacienda!*" Lita protested.

"Yes, Lita, it can," Ki assured her.

"Then we'll have to find a way to stop him from using the cannon," Jessie said.

Ki did not reply. His mind was busy considering alternatives while he watched the *rurales*. Guzman, limping badly, was waving his arms at his men, and though the distance was too great for his voice to carry, his mouth was working furiously as he hobbled around the spot where the wagon had stopped. The way the *rurales* were wrestling with the fieldpiece told Ki that they were completely unfamiliar with the weapon. That, Ki thought hopefully, might give him time to work out a way to forestall them before they'd done too much damage.

His eyes still fixed on the *rurales,* Ki muttered to himself, "What we need is what we don't have and can't get. Unless—"

"What did you say, Ki?" Jessie asked, turning away from watching the *rurales* trying to wheel the cannon around.

"Nothing," he replied absently, his mind still working at top speed. "Or perhaps everything."

"I don't understand," Jessie frowned.

"You will," Ki said. He turned to Lita. "Who treats the bulls when one of them gets hurt? Or when they get infested by ticks?"

Lita stared at him, bewilderment on her face. "Ki, why do you ask about sick bulls and ticks when Guzman is getting ready to fire his cannon at us?"

"I have a good reason, believe me, Lita. Who would be the one I'm looking for?"

"Why . . . Eusebio, I suppose. He's the *mayordomo,* he has charge of everything."

"Tell him that I want to talk to him, quickly. And I need a few more things that you can help me with—a yard or two of silk cloth, and some very strong thread. Do you have them?"

"I'm sure my maid has both. Shall I ask her?"

"Don't just ask her. Tell her to get the silk and thread and several pairs of scissors together, and bring them out to the building—I don't know what you call it, but it's where I spent my first nights. And bring two or three more women with you. But before you do anything, tell Eusebio I want to see him at once."

"I'll go along and help Lita," Jessie volunteered.

"Lita can manage her people without you, Jessie," Ki told her. "I need you to stay here and watch the *rurales*. Guzman may get tired of waiting for his men to get that cannon ready, and decide to attack us without it. But if it takes them as long to get ready to fire as it's taking them to get it off the wagon, maybe I can get together what I need in time to stop them."

Jessie nodded. "I think I'm getting a very shadowy idea of what you might be planning, Ki, and I certainly hope it works."

"So do I, Jessie," Ki said fervently. "So do I."

Ki hurried to the building behind the main house and waited impatiently for Eusebio to show up. He'd seen little of the *mayordomo* during the short time he'd been at the ranch; as the second in command after Don Almendaro, he spent most of his time supervising the activities of the hands.

"I need some things, Eusebio," Ki told the tall, aging man. "You must use sulfur here. And after looking at Don Almendaro's collection of guns, I'm sure there's a keg or two of gunpowder somewhere around."

"Of course, Señor Ki. Sulfur we use to treat the bulls when the tick season arrives, and there is much gunpowder." He cocked his head and squinted shrewdly at Ki, then added, "There is also a small amount of dynamite and some caps and fuse, if they will help you in your preparations."

"How do you know what I'm getting ready to do?"

Eusebio smiled. He said gently, "I am an old man, Señor Ki, and I have lived through three wars since my youth. I served with Juarez when he drove out Maximilian, and later I marched with Lerdo to help defend our land in his battles against Díaz. I have made more than my share of smoke bombs and grenades, and what else could you be planning to make, with the devil Guzman and his cursed *rurales* attacking us with a cannon?"

"Will you help me show the women how to make smoke bombs, then? I only need a few—five or six. And if there's dynamite, I won't need grenades. When you've got the women started to work, I'd like for you to cut two sticks of dynamite in half and put fuses in them. And I'll want matches too."

"Of course. I have some match-blocks that the herders use. How long do you wish the fuses on the dynamite?"

Ki frowned. "Fuse the smoke bombs very short. As for the dynamite, fuse two of the half-sticks for a quarter minute and the other two for a half minute."

"Those are very short fuses, Señor Ki. Are you sure—"

"I'm sure," Ki said firmly. "How long will it take you to do all this?"

"Twenty minutes, a half hour. The sulfur is in the shed next to this building, the dynamite and gunpowder only a bit further away."

Lita arrived within the next few minutes, with her maid and one of the women from the kitchen. Ki started them cutting the silk cloth into large squares. While the women began snipping at the silk, he took Lita aside.

"I'm going to need your landaulet," he told her. "It's the only closed carriage I've seen here on the ranch."

"Yes. Use it any way you need to, Ki."

"It may get ruined, or even destroyed," he warned her.

"I wouldn't care. It's old, and I don't like it anyway. I only used it because Father insisted."

Eusebio returned at that moment and interrupted them. For a few moments, Ki watched while the old man mixed

175

gunpowder and sulfur together and then showed Lita and the women how to spread a thick layer of the mixture on a square of silk and fold and roll the fabric into a tight cylinder, then wrap the cylinder with the heavy thread to hold it together. Satisfied that Eusebio could be trusted to finish the job, Ki went to the shed where the landaulet was stored.

Over the protests of the tottery coachman, Ki attacked the varnished wooden panel below the driver's seat. With a hatchet he cut a narrow slit in the thin panel, an opening wide enough to allow the reins to have free play and for the driver to see where the carriage was heading. Then, after instructing the coachman to harness the carriage horse, he went back to the roof.

"They've finally got the cannon off the wagon, Ki," Jessie announced as he emerged from the trapdoor. "It won't be much longer before they'll be shooting it."

Ki looked at Guzman and his men. The old fieldpiece was off the wagon now. It stood in the center of the road, its muzzle pointing menacingly at the *hacienda*. *Rurales* were bringing up bags of gunpowder and cannonballs and stacking them beside the ancient cannon, obviously getting it ready to be fired.

"They'll need a shot or two before they get the proper elevation," Ki said. "And we'll be ready to move in a few minutes. I'd feel better about this if I had real *nage teppo*, and could blind the *rurales* instead of depending on smoke bombs, but old Eusebio seems to know what he's doing."

"Can you disable it, Ki? Without flares, and out of practice as you are?"

"I'm rusty at it, but I'm sure I can get close enough to the cannon to put down a smokescreen with the makeshift *nage teppo* Eusebio's got Lita and the women making, and I've got dynamite to finish the job with."

"Ki, it's a long way from here to that cannon," Jessie protested. "Even a *ninja* would think twice before trying to cover it, even with the right kind of equipment."

"I think I can do what I've planned. I'll use the old landaulet to get as close as possible. I've fixed it so that the reins can be handled from inside."

"Then I'm going to be handling the reins!" Jessie announced firmly. "This isn't a one-man job!"

"No, Jessie. The *rurales* will be shooting at the landaulet from the minute they see it. It's too dangerous."

"Dangerous or not, I'm going to be inside it!"

Knowing when Jessie had made up her mind so firmly that he could not change it, Ki surrendered. "All right. Let's start now, then. By the time we get downstairs, everything should be ready for us to go."

After a last look at the *rurales,* who were now clustered around the cannon, getting it ready to fire, they went down the ladder to the second floor and started for the stairs. They'd taken only a step or two when Ki stopped short.

"You'd better put our gear in the landaulet, Jessie. Rifles, saddlebags, everything. We don't know what we might need. I'll have our horses saddled, and we'll put them on lead-ropes behind the carriage. After the job's done, we'll want to get away faster than that old landaulet will move."

As Jessie and Ki rounded the corner of the *hacienda,* the landaulet swaying gently, they heard the first cannon shot. They peered through the hole Ki had cut in the front panel, and saw the cannonball send up a spurt of dirt when it struck the ground a hundred yards in front of the *hacienda* and almost as far from the side of the building.

"They'll need two or three more ranging shots," Ki said. "With a little luck, we might get there just in time to spoil Guzman's plans, Jessie!"

Absorbed in the cannon, the *rurales* paid no attention to the landaulet for a few minutes. Then one of them pointed to the ancient carriage, and Guzman detached himself from the cluster of men around the fieldpiece to come to the front of the group and look. He waved to his men and shouted an order. Two of the *rurales* detached themselves from the huddle around the cannon and started for the picket line a short distance from the artillery piece, where the horses were tethered.

"Faster, Jessie," Ki urged. "I need to be closer before I become a *ninja!*"

Jessie was slapping the reins on the back of the carriage horse, trying to get it to move faster. Without taking her eyes from the road, she said, "I wish you had more cover, Ki. This ground is too bare even for a real *ninja* to cross without being noticed."

Ki had been thinking the same thing. *Ninjas,* the professional assassins of Japan who specialized in the art of approaching their victims unnoticed, wore skin-tight coveralls matching the terrain on which they worked. Dodging from one bit of cover to the next, creeping on hands and knees, belly-crawling when the ground was bare, these silent killers had perfected their skill through centuries of practice.

"I don't want to get too close to the cannon," he told Jessie. "And the *nage teppo* will give me enough cover to get to a place where I can throw the dynamite."

"Those *rurales* Guzman sent to cut us off are on their horses now," Jessie said.

"When they're halfway between us and the cannon, pull off the road and go across the range. The wind's coming from our left, so wheel that way when you pull off."

Jessue gauged the distance between the landaulet and the *rurales'* position with an expert's eye. "Three or four more minutes, Ki. Get ready."

Ki poised himself at the door opposite the *rurales'* position, and released its latch. Jessie kept looking straight ahead. The two *rurales* were midway between the landaulet and the cannon when she yanked hard on the left-hand rein, and as the carriage horse wheeled sharply, she gave Ki the word.

"Now, Ki! I'll pick you up on this side of the road when you've finished.!"

Ki jumped. The body of the landaulet shielded him from the eyes of the approaching *rurales,* who were interested only in watching the carriage and changing their course to follow it.

Because the *rurales* around the cannon fired the second shot just as Ki leaped from the landaulet, they were for the moment unconscious of their surroundings. Their eyes were on the cloud of dust raised by the cannonball, which had fallen only a few yards short of the *hacienda* this time, squarely in front of the entrance door.

He might as easily have walked up to the men around the cannon openly, on the road, Ki thought. Then, as the *rurales* moved to reload the fieldpiece and reset its range and elevation, Ki began using every scrap of cover and every subtle movement that his *ninja* instructors had taught him.

An instant before he reached a spot where he could throw the *nage teppo*, the *rurales* fired the fieldpiece for the third time. Before the smoke from the cannon shot had dissipated, Ki took one of the makeshift *nage teppo* from his blouse, snapped a match from the block he carried in his hand, and lighted the short-fused smoke bomb. The *rurales* were clustered around the cannon, reloading it. Ki tossed the *nage teppo*.

It hit less than a yard from the knot of *rurales,* and at once began pouring out a dense cloud of yellow smoke as the gunpowder ignited the sulfur folded inside the silk.

Ki had the second *nage teppo* in his hand while the match he'd used to ignite the first still burned, and within seconds the new smoke bomb was adding its blinding, choking fumes to those of the first.

Before a minute had passed, Ki had tossed four of the *nage teppo*, and the cannon and the *rurales* around it were engulfed in fumes and blinding smoke.

While the *rurales* were milling in blind confusion, rubbing their eyes to restore their vision, Ki lighted the fuse on the first half-stick of dynamite. He counted to eight, giving himself a six-second margin of safety, before throwing the dynamite under the fieldpiece.

Before its fuse burned the remaining seconds, Ki had a

179

second stick ready to throw. The first half-stick exploded while the second was in midair. The fieldpiece rocked with the blast, and the *rurales* around it were thrown like dolls, landing in a rough circle around the cannon, which now sat lopsided with one wheel of its carriage shattered.

Guzman had not been in the group clustered around the fieldpiece; he had been giving orders to the *rurales* forming into attack groups on each side of the road. The *rurale* commander wheeled his horse and galloped toward the cannon. The second dynamite blast spooked his mount and it began to buck. Guzman was thrown from the saddle, but he got up and began limping to his objective.

Ki had seen Guzman and waited to light the third fuse until the captain was at the fieldpiece, trying to comprehend the reason for the explosions. Guzman saw the dynamite when it hit the ground, and started running away, but the short fuse ignited the explosive before he'd gotten to safety. A chunk of the cannon's undercarriage caught him in the back of the head and Guzman sprawled to the ground, his skull crushed.

From both sides of the road, the mounted *rurales* were spurring toward the scene of the blasts. Ki waited until most of them had reached the shattered fieldpiece before throwing the last half-stick of dynamite. He started running toward the landaulet, no longer trying to hide. The *rurales* saw him, but before any of them could ride after him, the dynamite went off and men and horses were toppled like dominoes to the ground.

Jessie had gotten out of the landaulet and untied their horses the instant the two *rurales* who'd been sent to intercept her were drawn back to the cannon by the first explosion. She met Ki by the time he'd gotten halfway to the landaulet. He swung onto his horse.

"I don't think Guzman's *rurales* will be able to bother Lita or anyone else," Jessie commented. "Your *ninja* tactics weren't as bad as you thought they'd be, Ki."

"I'm rusty. I use the *ninja* approach too seldom."

"You did well this time."

They rode toward the *hacienda* for a short distance, then Ki suddenly reined in.

"Jessie, there's no real reason for us to go back to the *hacienda* now. Lita and her people there will learn to take care of themselves without our help. We've done our job, as far as stopping the cartel's concerned. Brad Close can take his punchers to the Tres Cerros ranch and drive his cattle home anytime."

"I was thinking the same thing, Ki. Unless you want to say goodbye to Lita—"

"No. Lita belongs to the past now. We live in the present, and need to be thinking about the future."

"We'll ride on into San Pedro and take the shortest way back to the Circle Star, then," Jessie said.

"Do you want to stop at Fort Chaplin?" Ki asked.

Jessie shook her head. "No. That belongs to the past too, Ki. I haven't any reason to go back there, either."

Ki and Jessie relaxed in the companionable silence that has no need for conversation as they reined their horses toward the road and began the long trip home.

Look for

LONE STAR ON THE TREACHERY TRAIL

and

LONE STAR AND THE OPIUM RUSTLERS

two more novels in the hot new
LONE STAR series from Jove

Also look for

LONE STAR AND THE KANSAS WOLVES

fourth in the hot new
LONE STAR series from Jove

all available now!

Longarm fans gather round—

LONGARM
AND THE LONE STAR LEGEND

The Wild West will never be the same! The first giant Longarm saga is here and you won't want to miss it. LONGARM AND THE LONE STAR LEGEND features rip-snortin' action with Marshall Long, and introduces a sensational new heroine for a new kind of Western adventure that's just rarin' to please. Jessie Starbuck's her name and satisfaction's her game... and any man who stands in her way had better watch out!

So pull on your boots and saddle up for the biggest, boldest frontier adventure this side of the Pecos. Order today!

—— 515-07386-1/$2.95

LONGARM

Explore the exciting Old West with one of the men who made it wild!